*Crouching low, with the stealth of an Indian on the war-path, Biggles made his way to the rear of the hut, where he sank on to his right knee and beckoned the others to join him. From inside the hut came the harsh voice of the* unter offizier, *answered occasionally by a softer tone.*

*'We shall have to wait until they come out,' breathed Biggles. 'Jump out when I do and be ready to shoot like lightning. If they drop their rifles and put their hands up, all right, but any move by one of them to raise his rifle, let him have it. It's the only way. It's either they or we for it, and they won't hesitate to shoot us. Ssh! Here they come.'*

Captain W. E. Johns was born in Hertfordshire in 1893. He flew with the Royal Flying Corps in the First World War and made a daring escape from a German prison camp in 1918. Between the wars he edited *Flying* and *Popular Flying* and became a writer for the Ministry of Defence. The first Biggles story, *Biggles the Camels are Coming* was published in 1932, and W. E. Johns went on to write a staggering 102 Biggles titles before his death in 1968.

**www.kidsatrandomhouse.co.uk**

# BIGGLES BOOKS
# PUBLISHED IN THIS EDITION

### FIRST WORLD WAR:
Biggles Learns to Fly
Biggles Flies East
Biggles the Camels are Coming
Biggles of the Fighter Squadron
Biggles in France
Biggles and the Rescue Flight

### BETWEEN THE WARS:
Biggles and the Cruise of the Condor
Biggles and Co.
Biggles Flies West
Biggles Goes to War
Biggles and the Black Peril
Biggles in Spain

### SECOND WORLD WAR:
Biggles Defies the Swastika
Biggles Delivers the Goods
Biggles Defends the Desert
Biggles Fails to Return

# BIGGLES
## and the RESCUE FLIGHT

## CAPTAIN W.E. JOHNS

### RED FOX

Red Fox would like to express their grateful thanks
for help given in the preparation of these editions to Jennifer Schofield,
author of *By Jove, Biggles*, Linda Shaughnessy of A. P. Watt Ltd
and especially to the late John Trendler.

BIGGLES AND THE RESCUE FLIGHT
A RED FOX BOOK 1 86230225 1

First published in Great Britain as The Rescue Flight: A Biggles Story by
Oxford University Press, 1939

This Red Fox edition published 2004

Copyright © W E Johns (Publications) Ltd, 1939

Papers used by Random House Children's Books are natural, recyclable
products made from wood grown in sustainable forests. The manufacturing
processes conform to the environmental regulations of the country of origin.

Red Fox Books are published by Random House Children's Books,
61–63 Uxbridge Road, London W5 5SA,
a division of The Random House Group Ltd,
in Australia by Random House Australia (Pty) Ltd,
20 Alfred Street, Milsons Point, Sydney, NSW 2061, Australia,
in New Zealand by Random House New Zealand Ltd,
18 Poland Road, Glenfield, Auckland 10, New Zealand,
and in South Africa by Random House (Pty) Ltd,
Endulini, 5A Jubilee Road, Parktown 2193, South Africa

THE RANDOM HOUSE GROUP Limited Reg. No. 954009

A CIP catalogue record for this book is available from the British Library.

Printed and bound in Great Britain by
Cox and Wyman Ltd, Reading, Berkshire,

# Contents

The word 'Hun' as used in this book, was the common generic term for anything belonging to the enemy. It was used in a familiar sense, rather than derogatory. Witness the fact that in the R.F.C. a hun was also a pupil at a flying training school.

W.E.J

# Chapter 1
# Peter Fortymore Receives Bad News

There was a pensive, almost wistful, expression on the face of the Honourable Peter Fortymore as, with his chin cupped in his hands, he sat at his study window and stared out across the deserted, moonlit playing-fields of Rundell School, where for five years he had been a pupil. The door behind him opened, but he did not turn, for he knew from the heavy, deliberate footsteps that the newcomer was his friend and room-mate, Dick Ripley, known throughout the upper school as Rip.

'Hello, Thirty, what are you doing?' he began, but 'Thirty' silenced him with a gesture.

'Hark,' he said tersely.

Rip joined him at the window and then stood still, his head a little to one side, listening. From far away, rising and falling on a light breeze, came a dull mutter, punctuated from time to time by a heavier rolling boom.

Seen thus in the moonlight the two boys were in strange contrast. Peter Fortymore—or 'Thirty', as he had promptly been dubbed when he had arrived from prep. school, since his elder brother, already at Rundell, answered to 'Forty'—was slim and dark, with finely cut features which revealed clearly his

7

aristocratic lineage and Norman ancestors. Rip, with his flaxen hair and blue eyes, was of the heavier Saxon type; yet, curiously enough, on the rugger field his ferocious rush was often outwitted by Thirty's swift, shrewdly considered tactics.

For some minutes they stood listening, both gazing towards the east whence came the ominous rumble.

'What is it?' whispered Rip at last.

'Gun fire,' answered Thirty in a strained voice. 'Listen to it. The wind is from the east; that's why we can hear so plainly to-night. There must be a big strafe on.'

'Forty's out there, isn't he?'

Thirty nodded. 'Yes,' he said. 'He's been out there over six months now, yet it seems only the other day that he was here with us. By Jove! Remember him knocking up that century last summer against Winchester? Now he is flying, fighting in the air—and still playing the game, I'll bet.'

'Yes, he was a grand chap,' admitted Rip. 'What was that motto you used to shout at each other at games?'

Thirty smiled. 'Thick and thin.'

'What did it mean?'

'Oh, it was only a free translation of our old family war-cry, meaning that we stick to each other through thick and thin. I wish I was out there with him. He's only two years older than I am, but I suppose they won't let me go into the R.F.C.* for another year at least. I've a jolly good mind to go now.'

* Royal Flying Corps 1914–1918. An army corps responsible for military aeronautics. Renamed the Royal Air Force when amalgamated with the Royal Naval Air Service on 1st April 1918.

'But dash it all, Thirty, you're not old enough.'

'I'm nearly seventeen. Heaps of chaps have joined under that age.'

'I know. I'm a bit older than you are, but my guv'nor wouldn't hear of my going yet. He's out there, too—a colonel in the Sappers. He told the Head—gosh! I forgot to tell you. The Head sent me to say that he wanted to see you in his study right away.'

Thirty looked up sharply, searching his mind for a possible reason for the summons. 'I'd better go,' he said. 'Wait here; I shan't be long.'

Three minutes later he knocked lightly on the door of the Head's study, and in response to the curt 'Come in' he opened it, and walked briskly towards the massive desk where he expected the Head would be sitting. He was, therefore, a trifle surprised to find him standing in the centre of the room, an unusual expression on his face; furthermore, his manner was odd, almost agitated.

'Come in, my boy,' he said, in a curiously husky voice, and stepping forward rested his hands on Thirty's shoulders, at the same time looking down into the keen, questioning face. 'Fortymore,' he continued, 'since you have been at Rundell, whatever your failings may have been you have always played the man. That makes my task . . . easier. Try to live up to that now. I have bad news for you.'

Thirty moistened his lips. A cold hand seemed to settle over his heart. Somehow, he sensed what was coming. 'Yes, sir,' he said firmly. 'Is it—Nigel?'

'Yes.'

'Killed?'

'I fear so.'

9

Thirty bowed his head so that the Head should not see his face. His teeth sank deeply into his lower lip. 'I won't blub,' he told himself fiercely. 'I *won't*.' Something seemed to rise up in his throat, choking him, and forcing tears into his eyes. He felt the Head's grip tighten on his shoulders.

'Bear up, my boy,' whispered the master unsteadily.

Thirty felt the Head's grip suddenly relax; heard him walk over to his desk and sit down. When he looked up he saw a sight he would never have imagined. The Head's face was buried in his hands. His shoulders were shaking. Thirty stared. A sense of unreality swept over him. The whole thing was a dream. It was preposterous—the Head, of all people, blubbing.

Suddenly the master stood up and blew his nose noisily. 'Forgive me,' he said huskily. 'If this is hard for you to bear, remember that it is also hard for me. One by one my boys are going out there . . . to the battle-field. One by one they fall. You have lost but one, Fortymore, but I have lost many. Your brother was Captain of the School the year before he left us, and in that capacity I saw much of him. A finer fellow never stepped into a classroom or on a playing-field.'

'Yes, sir,' choked Thirty, still fighting to keep back the tears. 'How did it happen, sir—do you know?'

'All I know is what I have learned from these,' answered the Head, pointing to three letters that lay on his desk. 'One is from the War Office, informing me that Nigel is missing, believed killed, and since you are his next of kin I am requested to break the news to you. The second letter is from your family lawyers, asking me as your temporary guardian—since you are an orphan—to inform you of your brother's presumed

10

death, and to notify you that the title passes to you. You are now Lord Fortymore. The third letter is a copy of a report from Nigel's Commanding Officer. It is very brief. After speaking highly of your brother's character and ability he goes on to say that Nigel's aeroplane was last seen by other members of the squadron falling out of control over Zafferville. A forward artillery observation officer watched the machine crash behind the lines. That is all, except that a German communiqué issued on the day in question states that five British machines were shot down by their airmen, all the occupants being killed. In each case the aircraft burst into flames when it struck the ground, so identification was impossible. It seems doubtful, therefore, if we shall ever know any more.'

Thirty nodded heavily. 'Thank you, sir,' he said in a tired voice. 'Have I your leave to go, sir? I should like to—think.'

'There is one last thing.' The Head opened the drawer of his desk and took out a letter. 'Nigel sent this, addressed to you, about a month ago, with a request that if—anything happened to him—I should pass it on to you.'

Still feeling that he was dreaming, Thirty took the letter and put it in his pocket. The Head held out his hand. They shook hands in silence, and then Thirty swung round and walked quickly from the room.

Rip was still sitting by the open window when he returned to the study. 'Close the window, Rip,' he said quietly.

'What's the matter?'

Thirty passed his hand wearily over his face. 'Nigel

11

has been killed,' he said and, slumping down into his chair, he buried his face in his hands.

There was a long silence. Rip sat very still, staring out into the darkness whence still came the distant mutter of guns.

At last Thirty looked up. 'I have a last letter from him,' he said, in a curiously even voice. 'He wrote it to me some time ago.' Taking the letter from his pocket he tore it open and read it from beginning to end. When he had finished he looked up again at Rip. 'Listen to this,' he said eagerly. 'I may be a fool, but somehow it almost gives me hope. I have a sort of feeling from it—that Nigel may not be dead, after all. Listen; I'll read the letter to you.

*Dear Thirty,*

*I hope you will never read this letter. Funny way of beginning isn't it, but you'll understand what I mean. The fact is, old boy, things are pretty hot out here, and although I hope I am not a pessimist it seems to me that sooner or later one is pretty certain to get in the way of a small piece of lead travelling in the opposite direction with considerable velocity. We are losing a lot of fellows—five in my squadron last week—but they are not all being killed. Which brings me to the point. Quite a number are being taken prisoner, although they are not to be blamed for that, because if a bullet knocks a lump off your engine you have got to go down, so if you happen to be on the wrong side of the line—well, it's your unlucky day. So many fellows are going West in this way that the War Office is sending an officer round—an ex-prisoner who escaped—to give people the tip what to do if they find themselves on the floor in Germany. The chap came here about a fortnight ago, and at the end of the lecture he asked if any one had any questions.*

12

*There were a lot of brass-hats\* present, and they smirked when I suggested that we ought to organize a sort of special rescue flight — the idea being to pick up fellows who were shot down. Having no imagination they only laughed at me, but, personally, I don't see why it shouldn't be done.*

*'From what I hear, the most difficult part of escaping is getting across the frontier. Scores of fellows are stout enough to break out of the prison camps, but what with dog patrols, electrified wire, double frontiers, hunger, and so on, few succeed in getting out of Germany. Sooner or later they are recaptured, when they are punished pretty severely for their efforts. Yet why need they have to get across the frontier? It seems to me that if certain big fields inside Germany were marked down, and fellows in the R.F.C. knew which they were, they could make for them when they found themselves on the wrong side of the lines (either before they were actually captured, or after breaking out of prison). The rescue flight would go to these fields from time to time to pick the fugitives up. It could do other useful things, too, such as making secret food dumps on which escaped prisoners could live until they were picked up. I say it is absurd that no attempt is made to rescue them. A fellow going out on a risky show might even make provision to be picked up if he was forced down on the wrong side of the lines. For instance, take my own case. You remember those holidays we spent together at Berglaken, when the guv'nor was Ambassador at Berlin? Remember the old hut in the valley where we used to sleep when we went fishing? I could hide there indefinitely. Within a mile of it, at the foot of the hills, there is a whacking great field big enough for a dozen machines to land in. If I went down I believe I could live on fish, corn, and fruit for a long time. Anyway, if*

---

\* Slang: Staff officers, with reference to the gold braid they wore on the peak of the service cap.

13

*one day I fail to return from a show, you will know where to find me.*

'*Well, that's all for the present, old boy. Don't be in too much of a hurry to get out here; it isn't all beer and skittles— as the troops say. My compliments to the Head and best regards to Rip and the others.*

> *Through thick and thin,*
> *Yours,*
> *Nigel.*

'That's what I call a sensible letter,' declared Rip when Thirty had finished reading. 'Pity we aren't in France; if we were we'd go and have a look round this place Berglaken.'

Thirty folded the letter and put it in his pocket. 'I'm going, anyway,' he declared.

'Going—where?'

'To France.'

'When?'

'Now.'

Rip stared. 'Are you mad?'

Thirty shook his head. 'I was never more sane in my life.'

'But how . . . ?'

'Listen, Rip,' said Thirty crisply. 'For the last three months you and I have been getting up at four o'clock in the morning, breaking out of school, and biking to the flying school at Barton to learn to fly so that we shan't have so long to wait before we are sent to France when we do join up. We can both fly, and the only reason that we haven't got our certificates is because we are under age. I've done eighteen hours' solo, and you have done nearly as much; plenty of fellows have gone to France with less experience than that. Heaps have learned to fly privately so that they can get to France quickly—Nigel told me so. All the same, I don't mind admitting that I felt a prize cad about breaking school when the Head was so jolly decent just now—but there, it couldn't be helped, and we are only doing it for the best. I have no parents to worry about me. Nigel was my only relation—apart from distant cousins who do not matter.'

'Well, I've only got my father, if it comes to that, and he's in France,' observed Rip thoughtfully. 'He'd give me a thundering good hiding, though, if I ran away from school and he found me in France.'

'Oh no, he wouldn't,' declared Thirty. 'He wouldn't dare. He could be court-martialled if he did. A senior officer daren't strike a subaltern, not even his own son.'

'What are you going to do—join up?'

'And hang about a training school for six months, waiting to be sent out? No fear. I've got a brilliant scheme; in fact, I don't mind telling you that I have been turning it over in my mind for some time. Now poor old Nigel's gone I don't seem to care much what happens to me, and that's a fact. This is my idea. The last time Forty was home on leave he got his promotion, so he dumped all his uniforms and got new ones with three stars on the sleeves. The old uniforms are in his room; I saw them there when I was home for the Easter hols. I'm going to put one on, go to the nearest aerodrome, get into a machine and fly it to France, and then report for duty at the first aerodrome I come to.'

'But you'd be spotted for a cert.'

15

'Don't you believe it. With thousands of officers walking about, who is going to take any notice of me?'

'But what would they say in France?'

'Nothing. They need officers too badly to worry about where they come from. I should have to pretend that I had been ordered to report, and hope that the C.O.* would think that my posting orders had got mislaid somewhere. In any case, even if I was found out, what could they do to me? Shoot me for trying to fight for my King and Country? No fear. Once I get to France they'll let me stay.'

'You mean us—not I.'

'Us—what do you mean?'

'You don't think I'm going to let you buzz off to France leaving me here swotting over Euclid and other rot, do you?'

'By Jove! Rip, do you mean it?'

'I jolly well do. When can we start?'

'Now; this very minute.'

Rip sprang to his feet and locked the door as Thirty climbed on a chair and pulled down a suitcase from the top of his locker. Throwing back the lid he took out an assortment of clothes.

'When we brought these here so that we could learn to fly without awkward questions being asked, we little thought how useful they were going to be,' muttered Thirty, as he struggled into an old grey sweater.

In a few minutes the change was complete, and Rip cautiously opened the window. 'What about writing a note to the Head telling him what we've done?' he suggested.

* Commanding officer

'He'd wire to the authorities to stop us,' protested Thirty sadly. 'We'll drop him a line when we get to France.'

'By the way, have you got any chink?' asked Rip suddenly.

'Why do we need money?'

'It's nearly a hundred miles to London, and it will take us a long time to walk.'

Thirty thrust his hand into his pocket and pulled out some loose coppers. 'Sevenpence,' he announced.

'I've threepence; it looks as if we shall have to hoof it, after all,' declared Rip.

Thirty threw a leg over the window-sill. 'What does it matter how we go as long as we get there?' he observed.

# Chapter 2
# The Adventure Begins

Twenty minutes saw them on the main road plodding steadily towards London. They hailed several cars going their way, but none would stop; with a lorry driver, however, they had better luck. In response to the boys' desperate signals he drew in to the side of the road, and only then did they see that he was in khaki.

'Gosh, we've stopped an army lorry,' whispered Rip.

'Will you give us a lift, driver?' pleaded Thirty.

'Where are you going?'

'London.'

'What for?'

'To join up.'

''Op in.'

In a twinkling of an eye the boys had squeezed themselves in next to the driver, and in another moment the lorry was once more speeding down the road.

Neither of the boys ever forgot that journey; it seemed interminable. On and on through the night they rumbled, sometimes meeting or overtaking marching troops, or lines of guns, or wagons. It was two o'clock in the morning when they arrived at the Crystal Palace, the driver's destination, where, with sincere thanks, they bade him farewell, and started on a long walk through the darkened streets to Mayfair, where the Fortymore town house was situated. They were deadly tired, and Thirty became more and more convinced that the whole thing was a dream. He wondered vaguely what Thompson, the caretaker, would say when he saw them, for it would be necessary to ring the bell to gain admittance.

The sky was just beginning to turn grey when, footsore and weary, Thirty exclaimed, 'Thank goodness, we're here,' and halted before a pillared entrance. His finger found the bell push and he pressed it steadily.

After a few seconds they could hear bolts being drawn. A key grated in the lock. The door opened, revealing a grey-headed old man with a dressing-gown thrown over his night attire. His eyes grew round with wonder as Thirty stepped into the hall. 'Master Peter,' he gasped.

'Quite right, Thompson,' admitted Thirty. 'This is my friend, Mr. Ripley.'

'But what in heaven's name, sir—'

'Never mind explanations now, there's a good fellow,' said Thirty firmly. 'Coffee, please, and plenty of it—and some sandwiches. While we're eating them kindly make up my bed and a spare one. Much as I regret the waste of time I shall have to sleep for a little while. You had better make up Master Nigel's—' He broke off, faltering. 'I nearly forgot,' he went on quietly. 'Have you heard the news, Thompson?'

'What news, sir?'

'My brother has been reported missing. Officially he is "Missing—believed killed".'

There was a moment of embarrassing silence. The old man muttered something incoherently, then broke down and wept unrestrainedly. 'Master Nigel, oh Master Nigel,' he sobbed. 'Such a lovable—'

Dry-eyed, Thirty cut him short. 'Thompson, please, to oblige me will you try to postpone your grief and give service to those who are alive.'

'But what are you doing here, sir? Why aren't you at school?'

'I'm going to the war, Thompson.'

'But how—?'

'It's no use protesting. My mind is made up. I will avenge my brother, if nothing more. In case there should be inquiries, kindly forget that you have seen us—you understand?'

'Yes, sir.'

'Good. Now please get us some coffee and prepare a room. We will share one.'

'Very good, sir.' With tears still trickling down his face, the old man departed on his errand.

'Come this way, Rip,' invited Thirty, leading the way upstairs. He opened the door of a bedroom, crossed over to a wardrobe and pointed to several uniforms that hung on hangers. 'There's our kit, Rip,' he said softly. 'Let us try to be worthy of the grand chap who once wore it.'

'I shall never forget that,' promised Rip, his lips quivering.

An hour later, having made a frugal and somewhat silent meal downstairs, they returned to the room, undressed, and got into the beds that Thompson had prepared for them.

'Call us at nine sharp,' was Thirty's last order to the old caretaker before turning out the light.

At half-past nine, having had a few hours' refreshing

sleep, the boys stood regarding each other speculatively, conscious perhaps for the first time of the seriousness of the step they proposed to take.

'They fit pretty well, I think,' observed Thirty, referring to the uniforms they wore.

Rip nodded. 'You know, Thirty, now that we have actually got these things on, I feel it is awful cheek to wear them without even enlisting, much less being gazetted*. We shall get it in the neck if we're found out.'

'We'll talk about that when the time comes,' replied Thirty evenly.

'What aerodrome are you going to make for?' inquired Rip. It was significant that although he was the elder he instinctively left the leadership to Thirty.

'Hounslow is as near as anywhere.'

'What sort of machine are we going to try to get hold of?'

'Any, but Sopwith Camels** if we have any choice, since we have done most of our flying on rotary engined Avros. Anyway, we'll get two single-seaters if we can; if not, it will have to be a two-seater. I don't care which it is as long as we get to France. Once we are across the Channel we shall be safe; the very last thing any one will suppose is that we are not officers at all, but two chaps who have run away from school. Why, even if we told any one I doubt whether we should be believed. Come on, let's go.'

* Formally registered as officers by having their names published in an official newspaper announcing official Government communication, appointments, dispatches etc.
** A single-seater British biplane fighter with twin machine guns synchronised to fire through the propeller.

At the bottom of the stairs, Thirty, with a curious smile on his rather pale face, pointed to a coat of arms that was painted over the front door. Below it, on a scroll, was a motto. 'Thick and thin,' he said quietly. 'That meant a lot to old Nigel and me. It's you and I, now.'

Rip nodded. 'Through thick and thin,' he said softly, and held out his hand.

Thirty clasped it, and then, as if ashamed of his display of sentiment, hurried into the hall where Thompson was waiting for them. He stared when he saw the uniforms.

'Lieutenants Fortymore and Ripley,' smiled Thirty. 'Oh, and Thompson, I'm afraid we shall need a little money. Do you happen to have five pounds about you? I'll give you a note to the lawyers in case—'

'Don't mention it, sir. I have some money in my room; I will fetch it.' He hurried away, and soon returned with five one-pound notes in his hand. Thirty gave two to Rip and put the other three in his pocket. Then he held out his hand. 'Goodbye, Thompson,' he said gravely. 'Thanks for what you've done.'

'But why are you doing this, sir?' protested the old man. 'Isn't one in the family enough—?'

Thirty pointed to the coat of arms over the door. 'Thick and thin, Thompson,' he murmured reprovingly. 'It's time you knew that.'

'Yes, sir. Of course, sir.' The old servant bowed his head as he opened the front door.

Thirty ran lightly down the steps and hailed a passing taxi. 'Goodbye, Thompson,' he called. 'Mum's the word, don't forget.'

'I shan't forget, sir. Goodbye, sir—and God go with

you.' Then, as if the old man could not bear to watch any longer, he hurried inside and closed the door.

'Hounslow Aerodrome,' Thirty told the driver.

'You going up to shoot down them blooming zeps*., sir?' inquired the taxi-driver eagerly, noticing the wings on the 'officers' breasts.

'Not to-day, driver,' replied Thirty easily, as he gazed in surprise at a passing Tommy** who had saluted him. In a hesitating sort of way he returned the salute; then he got into the taxi in which Rip was already seated. 'Gosh, did you see that?' he breathed. 'I mean—that tommy. He saluted me. It made me feel an awful hypocrite. We shall have to watch out for that sort of thing or we shall give ourselves away.' A peculiar smile spread over his face as the taxi moved forward. 'Well, here we go,' he said softly.

'By jingo! I'll tell you one thing we've forgotten,' declared Rip suddenly. 'What are we going to do for money? Five pounds won't last us long. Don't we have to pay mess*** bills or something?'

Thirty started. 'Gosh—yes. I'd forgotten all about that,' he muttered with a worried frown. 'I shall have to write to Thompson from wherever we end up at. All the same, we can't go on drawing off him indefinitely. Now poor old Nigel's gone I must have got a lot of cash in the bank, but the question is how to get hold of it. If I write to the lawyers, they'll give us away and we shall be sent back to school. Still, as you say, we can't live without money, and if the worst comes to the

* Zeppelin airships, a rigid construction airship used by the Germans over Britain for strategic bombing and reconnaissance.
** Slang name for any soldier of the rank of private.
*** The place where the officers eat and relax together.

worst I shall just have to write to them. Otherwise we might soon be court martialled for not paying our mess bills. It seems to me that our best chance is to try to put up a jolly good show as soon as we get to France; then, if we are discovered, they might let us stay out there. What a nuisance money is. Well, we can't go back now, can we?'

'No fear,' agreed Rip.

It took them rather more than an hour to reach Hounslow Aerodrome, where the first of the pound notes was almost exhausted in paying off the taxi.

'By Jove! Just look at them. Doesn't it give you a thrill to see them?' cried Thirty, pointing to a dozen or more aeroplanes that were standing on the tarmac. An engine was started up, and the sickly smell of castor oil* was wafted to their nostrils.

'Gosh, I'm trembling like a leaf with funk and excitement,' muttered Rip.

'Then you'd better let me do the talking,' returned Thirty. 'Only bare-faced bluff will see us through now. Come on.'

Together they moved forward towards the tarmac where several officers, some in flying kit, were standing about, and numerous mechanics were going about their tasks, for it was a fine day and a number of machines were in the air.

'Look!' breathed Thirty. 'Camels! Those are the machines for us if we can get hold of them. That's the type Nigel flew; he showed me the instrument board of his the last time he was home on leave. See those two with guns on? They must belong to fellows home

---

* The rotary engine of the Sopwith Camel used castor oil as a lubricant.

24

on leave. If that is so, it doesn't matter a bit about taking them because they will jolly soon be given new ones.'

No one took the slightest notice of them as they walked along the wide strip of concrete in front of the hangars* towards the spot where the Camels were standing. A little group of mechanics stood close at hand, a flight-sergeant among them. Thirty beckoned to the N.C.O.**, who stepped forward smartly.

'Whose machines are these, flight-sergeant?' he inquired blandly.

'They belong to two officers just come on leave, sir,' was the prompt reply.

'Ah, they're the ones we're looking for,' declared Thirty calmly. 'We're going to test them, to find out just what condition these overseas machines get in after a period of service.'

'Yes, sir.' The flight-sergeant showed not the slightest surprise at the statement or at the youthfulness of the two 'test pilots', for during the war pilots of eighteen or nineteen years of age were common, and many of them looked younger.

'Get the tanks filled up, flight-sergeant,' ordered Thirty calmly, and then, nudging Rip, he turned towards the nearest hangar. 'We shall have to see about borrowing some flying kit,' he whispered. 'It will be chilly upstairs, and we've a fair way to go. There should be plenty of jackets and things in the sheds.'

In this respect he was quite right, for there were several leather jackets together with other flying kit hanging on the walls or thrown across the wings of

* A structure for housing aircraft.
** Non-Commissioned Officer e.g. a sergeant or corporal.

aeroplanes. After a quick glance to make sure that no one was watching, Thirty picked up the nearest jacket, from the pockets of which protruded flying cap and goggles. Glancing round he saw that Rip had done the same, and together they hurried back to the tarmac.

'All ready, sir,' called the flight-sergeant.

'Listen, Rip,' said Thirty quietly, as he put on his leather jacket. 'We'll take off in a dead straight line and climb slowly. I'll go first and you follow me. Once we are in the air we are as good as in France.'

As he climbed into the cockpit, the feeling again came over him that he was dreaming. In spite of the reality of the scene he could not believe that he was actually getting into a war plane, bound for France. 'Switches off,' he called to the mechanic standing by his propeller, in a voice he hardly recognized as his own.

Breathlessly he watched the ack-emma* turn the big blade of the propeller. 'Contact, sir,' called the voice.

'Contact!'

The engine, which had not had time to get cold, started at the first attempt, and with exultation in his heart Thirty watched the mechanic run to the propeller of Rip's machine. Another instant and it was a gleaming circle of light like his own. For a minute or two he waited for the engine to get really warm, and while doing so made a quick survey of the instrument board. Satisfied that there was nothing he did not understand, he raised his hands above his head for the chocks** to

---

* Slang: air mechanic.
** Wooden blocks placed in front of an aircraft to prevent it moving when the engines are started. Orders to ground staff were always made by means of signals as shouted words might be misheard over the sound of the engine.

be pulled away; then, taking a firm grip of the throttle, he moved it slowly forward. The mechanic saluted to show that the sky was clear for the take-off. The machine began to move from the aerodrome, slowly, but with ever increasing speed; a moment later it was racing tail up across the short green turf. Thirty pulled the joystick back gently and the machine rose gracefully into the air. At a thousand feet, just beyond the boundary of the aerodrome, he glanced back over his shoulder and saw another Camel following close behind him. 'Good old Rip,' he thought joyfully. 'We've done it.'

# Chapter 3
# France

With Rip sitting close behind his tail, Thirty bored his way steadily through the atmosphere on a southerly course, and when, half an hour later, the Channel came into view, he experienced a new thrill. Beyond the narrow strip of sea, flecked with countless tiny crested waves, was a long dark shadow—war-stricken France, where a million men, crouching in shell-torn trenches, were engaged in the greatest life-and-death struggle in history. If only Nigel had been there—what a time they could have had together! A wave of misery swept over him, but he shook himself impatiently and looked down for something to distract his attention. Across the water, heading for the English coast, a broad-beamed boat was surging, leaving a long feather of wake astern to mark its course; on either side of it raced two slim shapes which even from his altitude he recognized as destroyers. 'It must be the leave boat*, and her escort,' he thought, and then dismissed the matter from his mind as the long, hedgeless fields of northern France rose up before him.

With Rip still close behind, Thirty crossed the coast-line and began closely scrutinizing the ground for an aerodrome. He also watched the air, hoping to see other machines carrying the red, white, and blue mark-

---

* The boat carrying military personnel home on leave to England.

ings*, for, if he followed one of these, he hoped it would lead him to an aerodrome; but although it was a fine day the atmosphere appeared deserted.

For another twenty minutes he flew on, now following a south-westerly course, which from memory—since he had no map—he felt sure would take him well behind the trenches and parallel with them. Then he glanced behind to make sure that Rip was following. What he saw seemed to stop his heart beating. So astounded was he that for several seconds he could only stare—and stare; then his heart appeared to burst into action again like a racing engine. Stretching for miles behind them was a ragged line of small, black, wind-torn clouds. Even as he watched there came a flash of orange flame perilously close to Rip's machine, followed an instant later by a bubble of black smoke which coiled and twisted as it grew swiftly larger. He ran his tongue over his lips which had turned dry. 'Great heavens!' he muttered in something like a panic, 'we're being archied**. The Germans are shooting at us.'

Before he could force his stunned faculties into action, there was a streak of flame not a dozen feet from his wing-tip, and something struck his machine with a vicious *whang* that made it quiver like a frightened horse. His reaction was purely instinctive; he flung the joystick over away from the shell-burst, but, forgetting to apply the necessary rudder, he skidded wildly across the sky. Another flash blazed in front of him

* The symbol showing a plane was British was concentric rings of red, white and blue—see front cover for illustration.
** Archie was R.F.C. slang for anti-aircraft gunfire.

and he careered through the smoke. The pungent fumes bit into his lungs and made him cough.

With his brain whirling, Thirty looked for Rip, and saw him steering an erratic course about a hundred yards away. 'We must be on the wrong side of the lines*,' he thought feverishly, but for the life of him he could not work out which direction he ought to take. Indeed, for a moment or two he could not think of anything; his power to reason seemed suddenly to have deserted him. He breathed a deep sigh of relief, however, when he saw that the archie bursts no longer followed him; they had faded away as swiftly as they had appeared. It did not occur to him that there might be a reason for this, but he was soon to discover his error of judgement. Turning, he joined Rip, who was circling as though he was lost, and, after having attracted his attention, swung his machine round to the south, realizing at last that he must have crossed the coast-line too far north.

At that moment his only sensation was one of thankfulness that he had escaped the horrible archie, but his relief was short-lived, for within a minute he became conscious of a peculiar sound above the noise of his engine. It was a harsh, intermittent rattle, as though part of his engine had worked loose and was vibrating inside the cowling. But when, an instant later, something struck his machine like a whip-lash, he jumped violently and looked hastily around. He was just in time to see an orange-painted, shark-like body whirl past him. Down and down it went, its wings flashing as the sun caught them; then it soared upward again

* The front line trenches where the opposing armies faced one another.

30

in a beautiful curve until its nose was pointing directly at him. At three points round the gleaming propeller there appeared tiny, jabbing spurts of flame.

Thirty could only watch, like a bird fascinated by a snake. 'He's shooting at me,' he thought—but still he did nothing. He became aware of numerous dark-coloured lines, like thick pencil lines, around him; they all seemed to start from the nose of the other machine. Vaguely he remembered Nigel once telling him something about special bullets called 'tracers*'. And it was while he was still wondering at this new phenomenon that something else caught his eyes. A drab-coloured speck, tiny, but growing swiftly larger, was falling out of the sky like a stone directed towards the enemy machine—for he had no delusions as to the nationality of the orange-coloured aircraft. Down—down—down it came, straight towards the German scout until it seemed to Thirty that a collision was inevitable. He recognized it for a Camel like his own. Fascinated, he could only watch. The rest seemed to happen with the deliberation of a slow-motion film. He saw the small brown object that was the German pilot's head turn suddenly; instantly the orange machine spun on its axis; then it jerked upwards; a tongue of flame burst from the engine and licked hungrily along the side of the fuselage. The nose dropped. A wing sagged, and the machine began to spin, then a sheet of flame enveloped it and it plunged earthward, leaving a great plume of oily black smoke behind it.

Thirty tried to swallow something that seemed to be stuck in his throat. He felt sick. In a daze he looked

* Bullets loaded with phosphorous which starts to emit smoke when fired, allowing the course of the bullet to be seen by day or night.

round for Rip, and was startled to see two Camels, not one, close beside him. The pilot of the leading one pushed up his goggles, grinned broadly, and then raised both hands, thumbs pointing upward. 'Thumbs up,' thought Thirty. 'He must be the fellow who shot down that German!'

With a sinking sensation in the pit of his stomach he realized that but for the new-comer it would have been he, not the German pilot, who lay in a heap of smoking wreckage on the ground. 'How did he do it, I wonder?' he mused. 'I shall never be able to fly a machine like that as long as I live.'

He was still occupied with these disturbing thoughts when he saw the Camel's nose tilt downward. He switched his glance to Rip, and then back at the strange Camel—or rather, the place where it had been, for it was no longer there. Pushing up his goggles he gazed around unbelievingly. Where had it gone? It took him a full minute to find it, far below and still going down. Then he saw the reason. At the corner of a large field, close to a straggling clump of trees, was a line of unmistakable buildings—hangars.

In a moment he was gliding down towards them. Twice he circled the aerodrome to make sure of the direction of the wind; then he glided low over the boundary hedge and landed, taxying straight on as soon as he was safely down to allow Rip plenty of room to come in.

With mixed thoughts he taxied up to the sheds, where the pilot of the machine which had saved him was standing lighting a cigarette. On the tarmac he switched off, jumped down, and walked slowly towards his saviour. 'Thanks,' he said nervously.

'What was the matter—guns jammed?' was the casual question that greeted him.

'Guns?' Thirty blinked, feeling foolish. It gave him another shock to realize that he had not even thought of shooting back when he had been attacked. What a hope he had of ever becoming a fighting pilot like Nigel! Despondently he confessed the truth. 'I'm sorry,' he blurted, 'but we've never been in France before; we have just come straight from England.'

The war pilot laughed, throwing open the collar of his oil-stained tunic. 'Ah, well, you'll learn,' he said. 'We're all hopeless at first, but I must say you were lucky to get here. I was just making my last turn before coming home when I spotted that marigold-tinted skunk plastering you. Well, he'll do no more plastering. Where were you bound for, anyway?'

'What squadron is this?' returned Thirty evasively.

'Two-six-six.'

'Why, that's the squadron we were making for,' declared Thirty, not untruthfully, since any squadron would have suited him.

'Good! We can do with some new fellows. The Boche* are keeping things lively, and I have some gaps in my own flight. My name's Bigglesworth—Biggles for short. I may need you to confirm my combat report, but first of all you'd better go and sign on. There's the orderly room** over there. Cheerio, see you later.'

Thirty turned to Rip. 'Come on,' he said, 'let's get it over. Our luck's been grand so far; it won't let us down now.'

Feeling more confident than he had been since their

_____
* Slang: derogatory term for the Germans.
** A room or office used for day to day squadron business.

33

wild escapade started, Thirty walked briskly towards the hutment which 'Biggles' had said was the orderly room. He knocked on the door and entered, with Rip close behind him. A little, sandy-haired man, with a terrible scar on the side of his jaw, was sitting at a paper-littered desk. He looked up as they entered. 'What cheer?' he said lightly.

'Lieutenants Fortymore and Ripley reporting for duty, sir,' said Thirty smartly.

'Fortymore?'

'Yes, sir.'

'You needn't sir me—I'm only the Recording Officer*; have you got a brother out here?'

'I had—he's missing.'

The Recording Officer rose to his feet and held out his hand. 'Bad luck,' he said quietly. 'Glad to meet you, Fortymore. Your brother was a stout fellow. If you shape anything like him we shall be glad to have you. Got your movement orders?'

'No. At least, we weren't given any papers to bring here,' answered Thirty truthfully.

'Never mind; I expect they've gone adrift somewhere. How did you get here?'

'We flew over.'

'The dickens you did. I heard a rumour that they were going to send new fellows over that way—much more sensible than boat and train. Just a minute, the C.O. will probably want a word with you.' The Recording Officer disappeared into an inner room, but was back in a moment. 'Come in and meet Major Mullen, the C.O.' he said.

* The officer designated to supervise the collation of all squadron records, responsible to Commanding Officer.

Thirty and Rip followed the Recording Officer into the C.O.'s office. To Thirty's surprise, a curly haired young man who could not have been a day more than twenty-five rose to meet them, a smile of welcome on his rather careworn face. 'Hello, chaps; welcome to two-six-six,' he said cheerfully, holding out his hand. 'I've been screaming for some new fellows for a fortnight. Know anything about flying?'

'Not very much, I'm afraid, sir.'

The C.O. laughed outright. 'That's frank, anyway,' he replied. 'Too many fellows come out here over-confident, and that's a mistake they seldom live long enough to discover. There is only one place where you can learn war-flying, and that's in France. Forget all you've been taught at home and start afresh. I believe in giving fellows a fair chance, so you won't go near the lines until I've passed you out. Put in all the flying time and target practice you can for the next ten days, then I'll see how you shape. You'd better go to—let me see.' The major turned and studied a chart that hung on the wall behind his desk. Thirty saw that it was a list of names, many of which, however, had been scored out. 'You'd like to keep together, you two, I suppose?' inquired the C.O.

'If it can be arranged, sir.'

'Nothing easier. You can both go to B flight. Captain Bigglesworth will be your skipper. He'll take care of you, for he's as stout a pilot as there is in France; do what he tells you and don't ever let him down. If you do,'—the C.O.'s eyes glinted ominously—'I'll shoot you myself. I must get on now. Go and find Bigglesworth. I think I saw him come in a minute or two ago.

Make yourselves at home; you'll find we're a happy family here. Goodbye for the present.'

'By gosh! That's a bit of luck,' said Thirty excitedly when they were outside again. 'Bigglesworth was the chap who saved us just now. I liked him from the moment I set eyes on him. Let's go and find him.'

'There he goes now, walking towards the sheds,' exclaimed Rip. 'Let's catch him up.'

Breathless, they overtook the flight-commander just as he reached the hangars. He heard them coming and turned to wait for them. 'What's the hurry—going home again?' he inquired brightly.

'We've been posted to your flight, sir,' replied Thirty enthusiastically.

The flight-commander regarded them thoughtfully for a moment without speaking. 'Don't call me sir,' he said at last. 'Ceremony doesn't cut any ice out here—and you'll soon understand why. How long has the C.O. given you to learn to fly and shoot straight?'

'Ten days.'

'Fine! Then let's sit down and have a chat about things in general. By the way, what are your names?'

'I'm Fortymore and this is Ripley. Thirty and Rip for short.'

'Why Thirty?'

'Because my brother was Forty.'

'Not Forty of eighty-four squadron?'

'That's right. He's—missing.'

'I'm sorry to hear that. Bad show. I've met him once or twice, and he struck me as being an exceptionally good scout. Ah well, that's the luck of the game. Pull some chocks over and let's sit down; there's no sense in standing when you can sit.'

36

Squatting on the low wooden chocks in the warm sunshine by the hangar wall, the flight-commander lit a cigarette and regarded the glowing end pensively.

Thirty looked at him curiously, finding it difficult to believe that his flight-commander had killed several men in mortal combat, for he was not much older than himself. Slight in build, his features were as delicate as those of a girl, as were his hands, which fidgeted continually with the throat fastening of his tunic. His deep-set hazel eyes were never still, yet held a quality of humour that seemed out of place in a pale face upon which the strain of war, and the sight of sudden death, had already graven little lines.

He flicked the ash off his cigarette with a little nervous movement, and then looked thoughtfully at the two boys.

'Now I'm not going to give you a lecture,' he began, in a soft, well-modulated voice. 'I'm going to tell you a few things for your own good. Nobody told me; I had to find 'em out for myself, which means that I must have been very, very lucky. In the ordinary way you might last a week; with luck you might even last a fortnight; if you pay attention to what I'm going to tell you, and survive the initial difficulties, there is just a chance that you might last until the end of the war. The more you know, the better chance you have of knocking down a Hun or two before you get knocked down yourself. That's what you're here for. First of all, until you know your way around, don't cross the lines under ten thousand feet, and even then stay within striking distance of home until you are able to take on anybody with a fair chance of getting away with it. If you are flying in formation don't leave it on any account—never mind what you see. It may be a Hun underneath—well, leave him alone; as like as not it will be a decoy to get you down so that you will be easy meat for the fellows who will be waiting upstairs. If you see anything suspicious, or something you don't understand, make for home as if the devil himself was after you. Always keep your eyes skinned. The air is stiff with Huns all hoping to get the Iron Cross, and it's new-comers to the game who give them their chance. Never stop looking for one instant—particularly in the direction of the sun; at first you'll see nothing, but in a week or two there won't be a machine in the sky that you won't spot. It's a knack that comes with practice. Don't worry about archie; its bark is worse than its bite and it seldom hits anybody. Keep away from balloons*, and watch ahead for balloon cables if you have to come home low down. More than one fellow has hit one—and aeroplanes don't like it. Remember, it's no use shooting at a Hun outside three hundred feet; it's a waste of ammunition—apart from which it tells the Hun, if he is an old hand, that you're green. Keep away from clouds; nasty people lurk in them waiting for careless people to come along. If you are meeting a Hun head-on, don't turn; it isn't done; make *him* turn; that's how we keep their tails down. Finally, if you are attacked by a Hun and things look grim, don't try to get away. Go for him as though you'd made up your mind to ram him; it's your only chance; it will give him the idea that you mean business, even

* Both sides in the First World War used balloons for artillery spotting and observation of enemy troop movements. The observers were suspended beneath the balloon in large baskets. Balloons were commonly called sausages by the R.F.C.

if you don't, and the odds are he'll clear off and leave you alone. Put in every minute you can at target practice. It's no use being able to fly if you can't shoot straight. It's better to be a rotten pilot and a good shot than the other way about. If there's anything you don't understand, about your machine or anything else, don't be afraid to ask me. That sounds rather a lot to remember, but it isn't much, really; in a week or two you'll be doing all these things instinctively, without having to think. Presently I'll take you up and show you the lines, and the best landmarks. Meanwhile, I've got to go and have a word with the flight-sergeant about my kite*; she's flying a bit right wing low. Go and get yourselves fixed up with quarters.'

A horrible thought struck Thirty. 'Gosh! We haven't any kit,' he muttered.

'What do you mean—you haven't any kit?'

'Well, you see, we flew over, so we couldn't bring any with us.'

'It will come up on a tender, I expect.'

'Possibly,' answered Thirty non-committally, catching Rip's eye. 'Meanwhile we have nothing to go on with.'

'No matter. You can get some small kit from Roddy, the mess secretary, and I can probably dig out an old suit or two of pyjamas. They may be a bit oily because on summer dawn patrols I sometimes fly in them—but that needn't worry you.' The flight-commander stood up. 'See you later,' he said, and disappeared inside the hangar.

Neither of the boys spoke for a little while. Then

* Slang: aeroplane

Rip regarded Thirty with a half-alarmed, half-amused expression on his face. 'Well, we've done it,' he observed in a tense whisper. 'We are actually in France, in a fighting squadron. This time yesterday we were at school. Jove! This is the greatest thrill of my life.'

'In a week or so, if our luck holds, I may get a chance to fly to Berglaken,' replied Thirty, in a voice that shook a little. 'That will be the greatest adventure of *my* life.'

# Chapter 4
# Into the Blue

For ten days, under the watchful tuition of their flight-commander, Thirty and Rip practised assiduously the tactics of war-flying, upon which—so they were assured—their lives would depend immediately they crossed the lines into enemy country. This consisted chiefly of gunnery, both with camera-guns* and shooting with live ammunition at a target set in a field not far from the aerodrome. The target in the first instance consisted of two old aeroplane wings lying flat on the grass, but when they reached the stage when they could hit it fairly frequently, Captain Bigglesworth—or Biggles as he was known to every one in the squadron—gave them a much more difficult mark to hit; nothing more than an old petrol can. This they were taught to shoot at from various angles, not the least difficult being a direct 'stall' immediately above it, which was one of Biggles's own specialities in the matter of attack.

Of general tactics they learned a good deal from conversations in the mess, where they listened with breathless interest to the stories of hair-raising exploits that occurred almost daily in that vague place known as 'over the lines' or 'in the blue'. Not infrequently Biggles was the leader of these exploits, sometimes in

* Literally a gun which takes a picture of its target instead of firing a bullet at it. Examination of the photo showed how accurate a shot would have been.

company with the other two flight-commanders, Mahoney and McLaren.

But of all their fellow officers the one for whom they formed the greatest attachment was a member of their own flight who invariably flew in formation at Biggles's right hand. He was an untidy youth with longish hair and a freckled face on which dwelt an expression of amused surprise. He was, they learned, a distant relative of Biggles's, and had come straight out from school and caused a minor sensation at the squadron by shooting down an enemy aircraft on his first trip over the lines. His name appeared on the squadron roll as Second Lieutenant The Honourable Algernon Lacey, but he was never called anything but Algy, even by Major Mullen, the C.O.

From the very beginning, possibly on account of their recent schooldays, a mutual friendship sprang up. Some of the older pilots sometimes showed signs of nerves, but Algy refused to treat the war as anything but a joke. The more his machine was shot about, the more he laughed, although on such occasions Biggles was apt to turn a reproving eye on him.

It was Algy who, on the eleventh morning after their arrival at the squadron, joined them on the tarmac in front of the flight hangar where they were waiting for orders. His Sidcot flying suit* was flung carelessly over his shoulder; in his right hand he carried the rest of his flying kit—helmet, goggles, and gauntlets. On reaching Thirty and Rip he flung his kit in a heap on the dusty concrete and eyed them both with mock seriousness.

'How are you feeling?' he inquired.

---

* A thick padded garment worn by airmen.

'All right,' replied Thirty. 'Why?'

Algy nodded sombrely. 'This is the great day.'

'You mean—'

'You're going over the lines—right over to where the big bad Huns are waiting to gobble little boys up.'

'You being one of the little boys?' suggested Thirty slyly.

A quick smile spread over Algy's face. 'Not me,' he declared. 'I used to be, but I'm a tough mouthful, now.'

'Is Biggles coming?'

'You bet he is. He's leading the show. Four machines are required to escort a photographic machine home; that's all; it looks like being a nice quiet party, so Biggles has decided to give you a taste of the real business. I'm making the fourth. We're to pick up the two-seater—a D.H.4*—over Douai, at ten o'clock.'

'Douai?' murmured Thirty. 'I've heard you speak about that place in the mess. Isn't there an enemy aerodrome there?'

'There certainly is. It's the little old home town of the Richthofen Circus**—the boys who fly the red Albatroses***. That's why the "Four" is going over to try to get a photograph of it. If we barge into any Albatroses take my tip and stick close to Biggles. But we may not see them.'

'Why not?'

'Because at that time of the morning they're usually

* De Havilland 4, British two-seater day bomber in use 1917–1920.
** Four squadrons of aircraft commanded by Baron Von Richthofen (nicknamed the Red Baron) the top scoring World War I fighter pilot who shot down 80 planes before being killed in 1918.
*** German single-seater biplane fighter with two fixed machine guns, synchronised to fire through the propeller.

43

at the far end of their beat—the other side of Savy. That's why the raid has been timed for ten o'clock.'

'I hope we see them, all the same,' murmured Thirty.

'You'll live and learn,' grinned Algy. 'That is, if you're lucky,' he added. 'Here comes Biggles; we'd better get started up.'

Biggles, in his flying kit, had come out of the squadron office and was walking briskly towards them. 'I suppose Algy has told you that I'm taking you over the lines this morning,' he began.

'Yes,' answered Thirty and Rip together.

Biggles nodded seriously. 'I shall keep out of trouble if I can,' he said. 'But if we do run into any I hope you'll try to remember what I have told you. Above all, don't lose your heads—and keep close to me if you can. Never mind what you see, and on no account leave the formation. If you do, it's ten to one you never get back to it. You understand that?'

'Yes.'

'Good! Then let's get away.'

Without another word Biggles turned on his heel and walked towards his machine, beside which two mechanics were standing.

The other three members of the flight made their way to their respective Camels, where they put on their flying kit, and after settling themselves in their cockpits started their engines.

Thirty, thrilling with a sensation he had never before experienced, looked across at Rip and, meeting his eyes, waved his hand encouragingly. Rip waved back. There was no time for anything more, for Biggles's machine, with streamers* fluttering from the inter-plane struts, had begun to taxi out towards the aero-drome. The others followed, and a moment later all four were roaring across the short green turf.

Once in the air they closed up, and after circling the aerodrome three times to gain height, the leading machine, still climbing, turned slowly towards the east.

Thirty gave his engine a little more throttle and moved up as close as he dared to the fluttering wing pennants of his leader. Once more he was finding it difficult to believe that he was not dreaming; that what he saw was really happening; that he was in an aero-plane flying towards the battlefields through a sky in which enemy machines were on constant patrol. Look-ing down he saw an expanse of brown earth, perhaps a mile in width, gradually merging into dull green on either side. Through the brown expanse that coiled like a mighty serpent across the landscape from west to east ran tiny zigzag lines, hundreds of them, making a cobweb-like pattern. His breath suddenly came faster as he realized that he was looking at the actual lines where two mighty armies were entrenched, grappling in a stupendous life and death struggle. From time to time tiny white puffs appeared, and drifted sluggishly across the brown expanse. They looked harmless enough, but he knew that they must be the smoke of bursting shells.

Remembering where he was, he looked up sharply, and with a guilty start saw that he had got out of position. Biggles was looking at him, beckoning him nearer with a peremptory gesture, so he made haste to

* Streamers were used to make it easy to identify the squadron leader or flight leader in the air.

close up again. Hardly had he done so than a little ball of black smoke appeared and mushroomed out not far from his outside wing tip. He no longer marvelled at it, for he knew what it was. They were over the lines, and they were being shelled.

Biggles flew straight on. He took no notice of the archie bursts that began to arrive in twos and threes. He did not appear to be aware of them. Thirty was, however—painfully so—as he realized what the unpleasant result would be if one came too close. Moistening his lips, he flew on, trying not to think about the venomous-looking little clouds of smoke with their fiery hearts. Presently, to his relief, they began to die away, as if the gunners had grown weary of their task.

Again he looked down. The country was absolutely strange, and he realized with a tightening of the heartstrings that should he by any chance find himself alone he would only have the remotest idea of how to get back to the aerodrome.

He caught his breath sharply as Biggles's machine suddenly rocked its wings. He knew what the signal meant*. Enemy aircraft were in sight. But although he craned his neck this way and that he could not see them. Then Biggles pointed with his gloved hand and he wondered how he could have been so blind. Perhaps a mile away, heading straight towards them at an altitude slightly lower than their own, was a machine which Thirty recognized at once. It was a D.H.4. But it was not alone. Trailing along behind it were six brightly painted aeroplanes. One was blue with yellow

* No planes had radio communication at this time so signals using hands or the plane's movements were the only way to pass messages between planes.

stripes, the bright blue nose gleaming in the sun; another was orange, splashed in a bewildering manner with black patches; another was lemon, with a purple zigzag stripe running down the side of the fuselage. The straight wings and V struts told him what they were—Albatros Scouts. One turned sharply, and he saw the black Maltese Cross* on its side. There was something so sinister about it that it gave him a queer thrill; it was not exactly fear, but it was something very much like it. Breathless, he watched the running fight draw near. That the D.H.4 was hard pressed was certain, both from the erratic course steered by the pilot and the feverish manner in which the gunner in the back seat handled his weapon, reloading with frantic haste when each drum of ammunition ran out and flinging the empty drums overboard as he snatched them from his gun.

Judging by the way he skidded wildly towards them, it seemed as if at that moment the D.H.4 pilot saw the four Camels for the first time. In an instant—it appeared to Thirty—they were in the thick of the enemy scouts, and he gulped as he swerved to avoid them, so inevitable did a collision seem. Never had he been so close to other machines in the air, nor had he seen so many in such a small section of the sky. Wherever he looked he saw an aeroplane. Then, with a gasp of consternation, he realized that Biggles had disappeared. So had Algy. Rip had begun to circle. In a fever of anxiety he looked around hoping to see the wing pennants of his leader, but an instant later the crisp chatter of a machine-gun behind him made him

* In the First World War the Germans used the Maltese Cross or simply a black cross as their identification symbol on their aircraft.

47

look back over his tail. For an instant he remained motionless as his horrified eyes fell on a blue nose so close behind him that the whirling propeller appeared likely to smash into his empennage*.

He did the first thing that came into his mind. He turned—and then jerked the joystick back convulsively as two machines raced across his nose, the orange Albatros, hotly pursued by a Camel. He recognized Biggles's machine by its pennants, and a wild hope surged through him that he might be able to follow it; but although he banked vertically, by the time he was round it had disappeared. A great plume of black smoke loomed up in front of him; from behind it appeared Bluenose, tiny flecks of orange flame darting from the twin guns on the engine cowling.

Thirty zoomed. His brain was in a whirl. Things were happening faster than he could think. Again came the venomous, fear-inspiring chatter of guns, and looking back in a panic he saw Bluenose again on his tail. In sheer desperation he looped. As he levelled out at the end of it something began to beat a tattoo on his fuselage; dry-lipped, he looked back, and in a sort of numb horror saw that Bluenose was still on his tail. He whirled round in the tightest turn he had ever made—but Bluenose was still behind him when he flung a lightning glance over his shoulder. Try as he would, he could not shake him off; and all the time came the intermittent tattoo of bullets hitting the machine somewhere behind him. He jumped violently as an unseen hand seemed to jerk at his sleeve; his

* General term referring to the tail unit of an aircraft, including the tail plane, elevators, fin and rudders.

altimeter appeared to explode, flinging its glass face into his lap.

From that moment a change came over him. A wave of cold anger surged into his heart as he realized that the other fellow was doing all the hitting. With his lips set in a straight line, he dragged the joystick back into his right thigh and held it there. The Camel banked viciously and remained in the turn. Bluenose appeared on the other side of a narrow circle; Thirty could see the pilot staring at him through his goggles. Enormous goggles they seemed. His head appeared to be all helmet and goggles.

In this position they remained for a good twenty seconds, during which time Thirty racked his brains to think of a manoeuvre that would bring him behind his opponent. In his anger he dragged the Camel round until it was spinning on its wing tip, but the other machine did the same and their relative positions remained unchanged.

Sheer impotence took Thirty in its grip; it was followed by a sort of savage desperation as he realized that so far he had not fired a single shot. He knew that the instant he straightened out Bluenose would be on his tail again, but he decided that it was a risk he would have to take; for the tail chasing could not go on indefinitely, with the wind blowing him farther and farther over the enemy lines.

He began his next move by shooting out of the circle. Bluenose flashed out behind him—as he knew he would; he heard the guns start their monotonous *taca-taca-taca-taca*. But before a dozen shots had been fired he had dragged his nose down in a spin. Five times he allowed the Camel to turn on its vertical axle before he pulled out, then looked swiftly around for Bluenose. He saw him at once, just pulling out of a spin, and he managed to get in a quick burst before the other saw him. Bluenose turned away like lightning, but Thirty for the first time had got him where he wanted him — in his sights. His hand closed on the Bowden lever* and he gripped it with a fierce exultation. His guns poured out a stream of lead. Bluenose turned, but Thirty, now exuberant, hung on to his tail, firing every time the other showed in his sights. Then a shadow fell across him, and he shrank as though expecting a blow. A Camel roared past just over his head. When he looked back for Bluenose the Albatros had disappeared.

Wondering where he had gone he flattened out and looked about him. To his utter amazement he could not see a single machine. The Albatroses had gone. The D.H.4, too, had disappeared. But as he watched, shaken by this phenomenon, a Camel swam slowly into view, pennants fluttering on its struts. It was Biggles. But where was Rip — and Algy? A cold hand seemed to settle over his heart as he looked down and saw a cloud of smoke rising from something that lay on the ground. Sick with apprehension he looked back at Biggles, who had now come very close to him. He had pushed up his goggles and was beckoning. Thirty looked at his face, and noted that he looked annoyed. Turning in the direction indicated by his flight-commander, he closed up behind him and followed him to the west.

Archie bursts appeared again, but a few minutes later the lines came into view, and shortly afterwards,

* The trigger to fire the machine guns, usually fitted to the pilot's control column.

the aerodrome. The nose of the leading Camel tilted down and he followed it, noting with amazement that in some extraordinary way another Camel had appeared and was gliding down near his wing tip. He recognized Algy's machine by its number.

Five minutes later he was standing on the tarmac wondering if the fight had really happened; everything seemed so quiet and peaceful. His knees felt strangely weak, and he noticed—not without annoyance—that his fingers were trembling. Algy had lighted a cigarette and was slowly taking off his helmet and goggles. Biggles was walking towards the place where Thirty was standing.

'What's the idea?' he asked coolly. 'Did you want to stay over there all day?'

'Well, I—I thought—I thought I was doing the right thing,' stammered Thirty.

'I told you to stick close to me if we ran into trouble,' answered Biggles curtly. 'Instead of which you went off and fooled around with that bluenosed shark.'

'Fooled around—' muttered Thirty incredulously. 'Why, I couldn't get away from him.'

Biggles's face broke into a smile. 'I'm not surprised,' he said cheerfully. 'I've seen that blighter before, and he's hot stuff. You were either pretty cunning or jolly lucky, I'm not quite sure which. He pushed off when he saw me coming back.'

Thirty was conscious of a feeling of vague disappointment; it seemed that he had not made Bluenose run for home, after all. Biggles had done it. 'What do you mean—when you came back?' he asked.

'I saw the "Four" nearly back to the lines, where I

51

handed it over to Algy and then came back to collect you,' Biggles told him.

'Did you see what happened to Rip?'

Biggles nodded towards the aerodrome boundary. 'Here he comes,' he said. 'Didn't you see him as we came in? He landed in the next field. He must have got his engine shot up, or else had his tank holed.'

Rip joined them. He was slightly pale, but smiling. 'I'm afraid I've bust my undercarriage,' he announced ruefully.

'I shouldn't worry about that,' returned Biggles evenly. 'You did well to get back, both of you. That was a pretty hot lot we ran into.'

'What was that machine I saw on fire on the ground?' asked Thirty.

'That was the fellow with the purple stripe. He was careless enough to give me a nice easy shot. I'll get you to confirm my combat report. Come on into the flight office; I want a word with you both.'

Wondering how he was to keep his eyes on his flight-commander in a dog-fight, Thirty, with Rip beside him, followed Biggles to the flight office. They found Algy already there.

Biggles closed the door and then faced the two junior members of his flight. He eyed them reflectively before he spoke. 'Just what do you two fellows think you're doing here?' he asked quietly.

Thirty felt the blood drain from his face. 'Doing here—' he echoed foolishly.

'Yes. Who gave you permission to wear those uniforms?'

Thirty felt something inside him go down like a lift; he looked at Rip hopelessly, and then back at Biggles, who was unfolding a small piece of paper which he had taken from his pocket.

# Chapter 5
# A Discussion in Confidence

Biggles, with the ghost of a smile playing round the corners of his mouth, smoothed out the paper, which the others now saw was a newspaper clipping, and handed it to Thirty without a word.

Thirty stared at the piece of newsprint with the dumb fascination of a bird under the influence of a snake, for in the centre of it was a head-and-shoulders portrait of himself, in his school clothes. Above it, in heavy type, appeared these words:

'*MYSTERY OF TWO SCHOOLBOYS*
*Lord Fortymore Disappears With Friend from*
*Well-known Public School*'

With sinking heart Thirty read what he already knew well enough—the story of his and Rip's disappearance from school following immediately upon the appearance of his brother's name in a casualty list. Various suggestions were then put forward as to where the two truants might have gone, concluding—rather shrewdly—by advancing the theory that they had run away to join up.

Thirty handed the paper back to Biggles, who tore it into small pieces and dropped it on the floor. For a moment or two he could think of nothing to say.

'How did you come to get hold of that paper?' he asked at last, haltingly.

'It was the merest fluke,' replied Biggles. 'The paper was sent to me from England because it happened to contain an account of a raid I took part in. Turning over the pages last night before throwing it away, I was not a little surprised—as you may imagine—to see your photograph. It was a bit difficult to see how you could have got a commission in such a short time, so I formed my own conclusions. Come on, you'd better tell me the truth.'

'Yes, I shall have to,' confessed Thirty miserably, and thereupon described the events from the time the Head had broken the sad news about his brother up to the time he and Rip arrived at the squadron.

Biggles's eyes grew round with wonder as he listened. 'Well, I never heard anything quite like that before,' he observed, as Thirty concluded his story. 'You two fellows certainly have got a cheek. But let me get this clear. Am I to understand that your real purpose in rushing out here is in the hope that you might, by some crazy scheme, rescue your brother—assuming that he is still alive?'

'That was the idea,' admitted Thirty firmly.

Biggles looked at Algy helplessly for a moment or two; then the expression gradually gave way to one of thoughtfulness. 'On the face of it, this seems to be the daftest, most hair-brained show I have ever heard suggested, and I've heard some fool plans expounded since I came out here. And yet . . . I don't know. Sometimes these crazy schemes come off. Tell me more about this idea of your brother's for rescuing prisoners.'

Thirty complied, going into the matter with some detail.

Biggles nodded when he had finished. 'I seem to

have heard something about this,' he said quietly. 'Somebody may have spoken about it in the mess.'

'The most important thing is, what are you going to do about *us*?' murmured Thirty nervously.

Biggles shrugged his shoulders. 'What do you suppose I'm going to do? What *can* I do? If I did my duty I should call the guard and put you both under arrest; and you had better understand that if I fail to do that I become an accessory after the fact—as they say in police courts—liable to pretty severe punishment myself.'

'Well—are you going to do that?'

Biggles smiled. 'No,' he said. 'There is a war on, and to my way of thinking that excuses a lot of indiscretions. Frankly, the part that concerns me most is this: if either of you two get killed I shall feel responsible. Really, you know, you are not old enough to be out here.'

'Fellows no older than us have come out. Captain Rhys-Davids was Captain of Eton* when he—'

'Yes, that's all very well,' demurred Biggles. 'There's no getting away from it, it's all a pretty kettle of fish. I'm dashed if I know *what* to do, and that's a fact. And this business about your brother. You are in my flight; do you suppose I can just sit back and do nothing, knowing that you are only waiting for an opportunity to tear off to somewhere in the middle of Germany with two of my machines? After what happened just now I don't doubt your courage, but, frankly, I doubt your ability to get away with such a show. If you two went

* Captain Rhys-Davids was Captain of Eton before he went to France and shot down more than twenty enemy aircraft, including the famous German 'ace' Werner Voss.

off I think it is extremely unlikely that we should ever see you again.'

'You needn't know anything about it,' suggested Thirty hopefully.

'But I *do* know.' Biggles turned to Algy. 'I can't help feeling that there may be something in this rescue idea,' he said seriously. 'I am not necessarily thinking about Thirty's brother; if the thing were properly organized there seems to be no reason why we shouldn't get quite a lot of fellows back. I've met several escaped prisoners, and they all say the same thing; it isn't anything like so difficult to get out of the actual prison camp as it is to get across the frontier.'

'That's right,' put in Thirty eagerly.

Biggles stroked his chin thoughtfully, staring at the wooden floor. Algy caught Thirty's eye and winked.

Biggles looked up. 'How far away from here is this place where you think your brother might be?'

'Just over a hundred miles.'

'That's the deuce of a long way. Few people, even old hands, care to go more than ten or twelve miles into enemy country. Don't misunderstand me. It's easy enough to get there; it's the getting back that takes some doing. I doubt if anybody has ever been a hundred miles over.'

'It's that very fact that makes it possible,' declared Thirty. 'The enemy will hardly expect to find us there.'

Biggles laughed aloud. 'Upon my life! You certainly know all the answers,' he said cheerfully. 'I'm bound to admit that there is something in what you say. Let us try to work the thing out. First of all, it wouldn't be much use your going in a single-seater like a Camel—

57

I mean, you wouldn't be able to bring your brother back even if you found him. You'd need a two-seater.'

'Of course,' agreed Thirty.

'Where did you reckon you were going to get one from?'

'Well, I . . . I don't exactly know. I had an idea I might borrow one from a two-seater squadron.'

'Great Scott! You've already taken two machines that don't belong to you. If you're going to punctuate your tour of service in France by going round pinching other fellows' machines, you're likely to become highly unpopular. But let us waive that for a moment. Let us assume that we *can* get a two-seater—a Bristol Fighter*, for instance; that would be the ideal machine because it can be thrown about like a scout. Suppose a two-seater went over—but wait a minute. I don't like the idea of a two-seater going over so far alone. It would be a prey for every Hun in the sky. An escort would be bound to brighten the chances of success. But even so . . . of course, if the job was done under cover of darkness it would be easier. If it were done in broad daylight thousands of people would spot the machines, and any attempt to land would instantly be telephoned to the Hun *staffels***, who, if they didn't catch the machines on the ground, would cut them off on the way home.'

'Machines—how many?' queried Algy.

'Well, I was thinking of a two-seater and escort,' continued Biggles. 'They could take off about an hour

* Two-seater biplane fighters with remarkable manoeuvrability. In service 1917 onwards. It had one fixed gun for the pilot and one or two mobile Lewis guns for the observer.
** German: Squadrons.

before dawn so as to arrive at the objective at the first streak of daylight. It need only be light enough to see to land. I, personally, don't relish the idea of trying to put a Camel down in the dark on a strange landing-ground. In the dark nobody would see the machines on the outward journey; they could climb up to, say, sixteen or eighteen thousand feet, and throttle back the moment it began to get light. If they did that, they might get down without being spotted. The biggest risk seems to be the delay on the ground. It isn't like having a definite appointment with somebody who we know is there; we should have to go and look for Thirty's brother.'

The use of the word 'we' did not escape Thirty's notice, and his eyes brightened at what it inferred.

'You say the only place where we could land is the best part of a mile from the hut?' Biggles asked him.

'Yes, but it doesn't necessarily follow that Forty would be in the hut; he might keep a look-out and run to the landing-ground when he saw us.'

'It doesn't follow that your brother is there at all, if it comes to that,' Biggles reminded him seriously. 'You should not overlook that point. I'm not trying to throw cold water on your hopes, but I think it would be foolish to buoy yourself up with illusions which may not materialize.'

'I haven't overlooked it, but all the same I shall feel happier when I've been over to this place, whether I find Forty or not. I'm sure that his letter meant that he wanted me to go if ever he was reported missing, and if I managed to get to France in the R.F.C. Until I've been I shan't feel that I've done my—er—'

'Duty,' suggested Algy.

'Not exactly duty. If I go I shall have the consolation of knowing that I have done all I can.'

'Yes, I quite see how you feel about it,' said Biggles, softly. 'I should feel the same way about it myself.'

'Am I to understand that you are not going to have us arrested, then?'

'I'm going to forget that I ever saw that newspaper cutting.'

'And you won't stop me from trying to get to Berglaken?'

'I'm not going to let you try to get there alone, if that's what you mean. My common sense tells me that you are so new to the game that you'd stand a much better chance of success if some one of experience went with you—a couple of fellows like—er—me and Algy.'

Thirty's eyes glowed his thanks. Suddenly they moistened. 'It's awfully decent of you—to do—this for me,' he murmured huskily.

'Rot!' interrupted Biggles tersely. 'If you want to know the truth, my feeling in this matter is that you've put up such a good show getting out here as you did that I should be the last one to send you back to school. I'll help you to find your brother, if he is still alive. On consideration, the scheme is not so hair-brained as it appeared at first sight, due chiefly to the fact, as you have said, that the enemy will hardly expect a British formation so far over their own country. Anyway, the whole thing is a brand new idea, and it is the new idea that gets away with it. I fancy the whole thing will boil down to a matter of perfect timing; I mean, getting there without being seen. Let me think about it for a few hours. There is the matter of the two-seater to be arranged also. I'll slip over to the pool at Amiens and see if I can fix it. We'll have another discussion to-night in my room after dinner. You can wash out now. After lunch you'd both better start practising forced landings. I shall have to make out my report now, or the C.O. will wonder what I'm up to.'

# Chapter 6
# The Great Adventure

Two days after the events narrated in the previous chapter Thirty and Rip picked up their flying kit and made their way towards the hangars.

It was dark, although a nearly full moon cast an eerie light over the sombre landscape, for the hour was three o'clock in the morning. Silence, broken only by the distant mutter of guns, and the sinister *pour-vous, pour-vous* of a Mercedes motor as a German bomber droned on an unknown mission, hung over the deserted aerodrome. Only these sounds, and an occasional flash of greenish light from the direction of the lines, where anxious sentries were keeping watch by the aid of star-shells*, told of the unceasing struggle that was being waged only a few miles away.

Neither of the boys spoke. Thirty was almost overcome by the profound importance of the occasion. He had passed the stage of being excited. Every nerve in his body felt like a steel spring, coiled, tense, straining for relief. For him a dream, an almost unbelievable dream, was coming true; he was going to keep a tryst, a sacred tryst, a vague assignation with some one who meant more to him than any one else in the world, yet who might not be alive. It is hardly to be wondered at that, as he walked towards the silent, camouflaged

* An explosive projectile, designed to burst in the air and light up the enemy's position.

hangars, looking enormous in the half light, he was obsessed by a feeling of unreality. Everything was as dim, as nebulous, as a barely remembered memory— the sheds, the ghostly silhouettes of the machines standing in front of them, the flying kit he carried—even himself. Little wonder that he was in no mood for speech.

The plan of operations, as finally decided upon by Biggles, was this.

Three machines were to take part in the rescue flight, a Bristol Fighter and two Camels. The two scouts were to be flown by Biggles and Algy, since they would be better able than the others to put up a vigorous resistance should the formation be attacked on the return journey; moreover, as they had had more experience they would be better qualified to land them in circumstances that would certainly be difficult. Thirty and Rip were to go in the Bristol, Thirty to act as pilot and Rip as gunner. Biggles had pointed out that although the Bristol was only a two-seater, Thirty and Rip were so slight in build and weight that they did not together weigh much more than one fully-grown man; the machine, carrying no bombs, would therefore be able to carry a third person if necessity arose—as, naturally, they all hoped it would. Two persons in the rear cockpit would, of course, be a tight fit, but Biggles decided that as it was possible it would be better than taking an extra machine.

Thirty had a shrewd suspicion that the real reason for this arrangement was the doubt in Biggles's mind as to the likelihood of there being a passenger to bring back. And in this he was right. In his heart Biggles could not help but feel that they would come back empty-handed. Had they been certain that Forty was alive the whole thing would have been different; so it would have been had they merely to pick up a waiting passenger from a distant objective. But the chances were that Forty was dead. Without saying anything to Thirty, Biggles had made inquiries at Forty's squadron, and had learned—to regard the matter in its most optimistic light—that there was no reason to suppose that Forty was still alive.

The three machines were to take off at two-minute intervals and fly a compass course at a pre-arranged speed and altitude to the destination. There was no question of flying in formation; the darkness made that impossible. But by pursuing the same course at the same speed, at different heights so that there would be no possibility of collision, they ought to arrive over the objective at break of dawn within sight of each other. They would then take up formation, and, cutting their engines, glide down and land. After that, everything would depend upon circumstances. 'Anything might happen,' as Biggles put it, tersely, and, no doubt, correctly.

When Thirty and Rip reached the tarmac neither Biggles nor Algy had arrived. They were, in fact, a few minutes early. Biggles's mechanic, Sergeant Smyth, was there, with two or three ack-emmas. Thirty, restless with impatience, passed the time by putting on his flying kit, and a few moments later Biggles and Algy arrived.

'Everything ready, Sergeant?' asked Biggles.

'All ready, sir,' was the crisp response.

'Good! Then you may as well start up, Sergeant. We are five minutes in front of schedule; still, so much the

better, that will give us plenty of time to warm up.'
Biggles turned to Thirty and Rip. 'On a show like this,'
he said quietly, 'everything depends upon carrying out
orders to the letter. Any departure from a fixed plan—
except, of course, through circumstances beyond control—means increased risks for others. You are absolutely clear about everything? If not, now is the time to
speak.'

'Everything is quite clear,' declared Thirty. 'Do you
mind my asking if the C.O. knows what we are doing?
I saw you talking to him last evening.'

'I asked permission to go out on a special mission,
and he gave it, imagining no doubt, that as a flight-
commander I had a sense of responsibility. If he knew
just what we proposed doing he would jump up in the
air so high that he would hit his head on the ceiling.
I've taken Mahoney into my confidence; he'll explain
to the C.O. what we tried to do—if we don't come
back. And I may as well say this. The best thing that
could happen—apart from your brother—is that we
make a success of this show. Afterwards it would be
unlikely that headquarters would send you back home.
These shows are always the same. Succeed—and you
get a decoration, a pretty little cross. Fail—and you
might as well get another sort of cross—a wooden one.
Frankly, I think your only chance of being allowed to
stay out here—getting a commission in the field—is to
put up a good show. Well, I think that's all.' Biggles
looked at his luminous wrist watch. 'Time's up; let's
get away,' he announced, crisply.

Biggles and Algy walked towards their respective
machines for they had all been standing near the
Bristol. Thirty looked at Rip. Then, moved by some

65

impulse, he held out his hand. ' "Thick and thin", old boy,' he said in a low voice.

' "Thick and thin",' echoed Rip softly, and in another moment they were climbing into their seats.

The engines had already been started and warmed up by the mechanics, so there was no delay. The Bristol was to be the first to take off. A glance behind to make sure that Rip was ready, and Thirty's left hand closed over the throttle. The roar of the engine shattered the silence. The Bristol surged forward with ever-increasing speed; a few slight bumps and it was in the air, climbing slowly towards the lines.

At two thousand feet, still climbing, Thirty touched his rudder-bar and swung the snub nose round to its allotted course; then he settled himself back for the long flight ahead. But he was not to remain undisturbed for long. A few minutes later the white beam of a searchlight stabbed the sky, flashing its question with the 'letter of the night' in the Morse code. The letter was B, one long flash followed by three short ones. Rip, in the back seat, was ready. His signal pistol roared, and the 'colour of the night', red changing to blue, soared like a meteor through the starry sky*.

* For the benefit of those who are unaware of their use in the First World War, the 'colour of the night' and 'letter of the night' must be explained. Briefly, it was a method employed by both sides to establish identification at night—when the aircraft could not, of course, be seen—for the benefit of the archie gunners. Every night the searchlights adopted a letter, which could be signalled in the Morse code by flashing the beam. Night-flying pilots carried signal flares of a pre-arranged colour—the colour of the night. When the searchlight units heard an aeroplane in the air, they flashed the letter, which was as good as saying, 'Who are you?' The pilot—if he were a British pilot—fired the appropriate colour and passed on unmolested. If he failed to do so he would be taken for an enemy, and shelled, for, naturally, a German pilot could not know the correct colour.

The questing beam disappeared with the peculiar suddenness of its kind, and the Bristol roared on, unmolested by the waiting archies.

A few moments later, however, another beam flashed, this time from some distance ahead. Another joined it, and another, the three wedges of white light 'scissoring' in a criss-cross pattern as they tried to get the night-bird in their grip. They gave Thirty the impression of giant forceps, trying to close on him and crush him to death.

A number of dull crimson sparks some distance away attracted his attention, and he looked at them curiously; but when, shortly afterwards, a vivid orange flash lacerated the indigo sky not far away, and he heard the dull *whoof* of an explosion, he knew that the sparks were bursting archie shells in a new guise. He perceived quickly that those which burst at a distance were crimson, while those that were nearer were various shades of red from scarlet to orange. Few shots came near him, however; presently the waving searchlight beams were left behind and he bored into the eastern sky with more confidence.

Knowing that they were either over Germany or very near to it, Thirty looked down with fresh curiosity, but he could see little. He appeared to be flying across the top of an immense bowl, the bottom of which was submerged in vague blue-black shadows. A broad river which he knew must be the Rhine coiled like a piece of silver tape across the mysterious depths. Here and there a spark of yellow light, from the window of an isolated dwelling, glowed in the darkness. That was all. With frequent glances at his compass to check his course, he flew on, conscious of a strange sense of power. Below were thousands of human beings, each one an enemy, yet not one could stop him, he thought.

He looked at his watch and saw that he had been in the air for fifty minutes. The sky ahead had begun to pale, and the stars to lose their brilliance, and he knew that dawn was not far off. He stared about him, hoping to see the two Camels, but the light was as yet too dim for him to see any distance and there was no sign of them in his proximity. The Bristol was alone in a lonely world of its own. Twisting his body in the small space available, he looked back at Rip, thinking, perhaps, to restore their mutual confidence by a nod, or a signal. But Rip was looking back over the Bristol's tail; with his left hand resting on the gun mounting, and his right hand on the edge of the cockpit, he stood motionless; he might have been a dummy, so still did he stand.

The sky to the east was now turning to pale lavender, and Thirty looked around anxiously for the Camels, for he knew that he must be nearing Berglaken; already he could see the pine-covered hills ahead, with drifts of pale grey morning mist lying in the valleys. His hand moved to the throttle, and simultaneously a Camel appeared at his starboard wing-tip with a suddenness that made him catch his breath. He stared at it unbelievingly, for a moment before he could have sworn that he was alone in the sky. He had no idea of where it had come from, and a wave of depression ran over him as he realized that it might so easily have been a Boche plane. 'My goodness! I've certainly got a lot to learn yet,' he thought gloomily. He was not surprised to see a second Camel swim into view on the other side of him; it was rather like a goldfish floating in a bowl. Looking at it closely he was somewhat concerned to

68

see Algy's mouth opening and shutting as though he were gasping for breath; Algy looked across at him, and raised his left hand in a gesture that was something between a salute and a wave. With a mild shock Thirty understood the facial contortions: Algy was singing. Then, suddenly, his mouth closed, and he pointed. Following the direction Thirty saw that Biggles's Camel was sinking into the void, and he knew that he had cut his engine. Swiftly he retarded his throttle and, as the roar of the engine died away, pushed the joystick forward. The Bristol's blunt nose sagged, and the machine began to lose height.

As he glided down Thirty studied the ground; it all looked strange and mysterious, and at first he could recognize nothing; but as he continued to stare he picked up his first landmark—two small lakes connected by a narrow canal that gave the whole thing the appearance of a dumb-bell—he remembered it perfectly, for he had fished in the lakes many times. Once having got his bearings he was able to pick up other features he knew—a narrow road which wound through the wooded hills, ruins of a once noble *schloss**, and a brook. He knew, therefore, just where to look for the proposed landing-place, and smiled his relief to see that it was still there; he did not, of course, expect to find that it had gone, but it gave him a queer thrill to see that it was unchanged, that it was exactly as he had visualized it. The hut, however, he could not see, for the valley in which it stood was still enveloped with ground-mist.

Carefully, flying no faster than was necessary in order to reduce noise to a minimum, Thirty nosed

* German: castle.

down towards the landing-ground. The needle of his altimeter crept back, and the panorama began to assume a more normal appearance. It all looked very peaceful. As far as he could see there was not a single vehicle on the one road that threaded its way across it; this did not surprise him, for, apart from the very early hour, the district was a lonely one, because the hills made it unsuitable for agricultural purposes.

Slowly the Bristol sank towards the green turf, Thirty tense in his seat, knowing how much depended on a good landing. A blunder resulting in a broken under-carriage would see him and Rip stranded in the heart of the enemy's country, with a likelihood of their being shot as spies if they were captured. Apart from which, the discovery of a British machine by one of the char-coal-burners who lived in the hills would be all that was necessary to start a hue and cry, so that far from rescuing Forty, if he were in the hut, they would only make his hiding-place untenable.

But Thirty's fears were soon set at rest; the Bristol bumped, swayed a little over the uneven ground, and then trundled to a standstill almost in the shadow of the firs that flanked the open space on which he had landed.

With a musical hum of wind in their wires the two Camels came in together. Neither Biggles nor Algy blipped his engine; they both allowed their machine to run to a stop wherever they would, although in neither case were they far away.

Thirty and Rip had already jumped out and, in accordance with the plan, as soon as Biggles's machine was on the ground they ran across to it and helped him to drag it as far into the trees as was possible, where it was left with its nose pointing in the direction of the open heath, ready for a quick take-off should it become necessary. Algy had joined them, and all four now handled the other two machines in the same way. Not until the three machines stood in line did they pause from their activities.

'Listen!' said Biggles quietly.

They all stood still for two or three minutes, but the only sounds were the chirping of birds in the trees, and the babble of an unseen brook somewhere near at hand.

'Good!' said Biggles at last, satisfied that all was well. 'I think we've pulled off the first part as well as could be expected; we couldn't have made less noise. Now for the hut. Have your automatics ready, but remember, no shooting unless we run into armed men. Peasants, or labourers, or whoever live in these woods, are not likely to attack us; if they see us they'll be more scared than we shall be; but if we are unlucky enough to run into any Boche troops, why, then, shoot out and shoot to kill. They will, for we are just as much at war here as if we were in the trenches. Rip, you'll stay here. You remember what you are to do?'

'Yes.'

'What?'

'Stand by and keep guard and be ready for a quick start-up. If I hear shouting, or if you shoot, I am to start up the Bristol and take station by the prop*. of your machine ready to swing it. If the machines are discovered I am to fire three quick shots.'

'Right,' said Biggles. 'Let's go. Lead the way, Thirty.'

* Slang: propeller.

# Chapter 7
# Neck or Nothing

Closely followed by Biggles and Algy, Thirty struck off at as fast a pace as was compatible with caution along the base of the hills, but before he had gone very far he turned sharply to the right into a deep valley, through which gurgled a brook, with dense fir-clad banks on either side rising to a height of two or three hundred feet.

'It's rough going,' he warned the others. 'Our best plan is to follow the brook. There is no path.'

Biggles nodded without speaking, and they went on.

As Thirty had said, the going was rough, and it was clear that the only living creatures that normally moved in the valley were the rabbits whose burrows were everywhere, and the speckled trout that darted for cover under the overhanging banks as the airmen splashed along the boulder-strewn bed of the stream.

'I used to come here after these fish,' explained Thirty.

'You're after something more important than fish now,' Biggles told him. 'Watch your step amongst these rocks; a twisted ankle wouldn't make things any easier.'

Nothing more was said for perhaps ten minutes, by which time they had climbed a spur of rock that barred further progress along the brook. Lying on the top, Thirty parted the heather that sprouted out of every cranny, and pointed.

'There's the hut,' he said in a voice that had an oddly dramatic ring behind it.

Keeping under cover, the others crept forward and looked over Thirty's shoulders.

They saw a valley very much like the one through which they had just come, except that it was not quite so rough and the banks were not so steep. The hut, a small, square, dilapidated building, rested a little way up the hill-side, making a pleasing feature in what was a very pretty piece of scenery.

'Well, if looks are anything to go by, it's deserted,' decided Biggles, referring, of course, to the hut.

'Even if he is there, it is not unlikely he is out at this hour of the morning,' Thirty pointed out.

'Then we'll push along and set all doubt at rest,' declared Biggles. 'Once we get to the hut we shall soon find out if any one has been living in it.'

He half rose, preparatory to moving on, but instantly dropped flat again as a sound floated down the valley.

'What was that?' jerked out Algy.

'Sounded like some one shouting—calling a dog,' whispered Thirty, the colour going from his face.

'A gamekeeper, perhaps,' suggested Biggles. 'Do they have gamekeepers here, Thirty?'

'Yes; there are wild boars in the forest, and they mark them down for hunting.'

Further speculation was cut short by the arrival on the scene of a party of new-comers, and the mystery of the call was explained. On the face of it, it looked as if the attempt at rescue had come to an abrupt end, for the party consisted of six men. In front, with a hound dragging on its lead, was a green-coated game warden, a feather curling jauntily from his cap and a brass hunting horn swinging at his side.

But it was not the mere sight of the gamekeeper that caused the last vestige of colour to drain from Thirty's face, leaving it a chalky grey; it was those who followed close behind him—five German soldiers with an *unter offizier**—judging by his manner—at their head. They wore the regulation grey uniforms, and, with the exception of the *unter offizier*, who wore a *pickelhaube*, the well-known coal-scuttle steel helmets. Down the hill-side they came, scrambling round a shoulder of rock in such a way that their objective was at once obvious. It was the hut.

'And to think we got so near,' moaned Thirty in a voice of anguish; 'and after all this time, to arrive just five minutes too late.'

'All right, don't lose your head,' replied Biggles, evenly. 'You ought to be dancing for joy.'

'Dancing for— Why?'

'Don't you realize what that little party means? It means the most important thing of all. Your brother *is still alive*—at least, that's how it looks to me. The gamekeeper must have spotted him and fetched the troops. Don't worry. The game is still ours if we keep cool. We know they are there—*but they don't know we are*. That's our trump card. Now let us see if we can play it. This way—quickly.'

Without a glance behind to see if the others were following, Biggles was off down the hill-side to get round the obstacle that lay across their path, jumping nimbly from rock to rock and ducking under the droop-

---

* German non-commissioned officer e.g. a Corporal or Sergeant.

ing branches of the sombre firs that often stood in his path. His automatic was in his hand.

The others followed. Up the opposite bank they clambered, pulling themselves up by any hand-hold that offered, until they were in a thick belt of trees, running over a sloping bed composed of generations of fir needles on which their feet made no noise. Under cover of the trees they ran on until they were, as near as they could judge, opposite the hut, where Biggles slowed down and crept forward. The others followed at his heels, and were just in time to see the second act of the drama that was being enacted in the sylvan scene.

Another actor had appeared. Moving cautiously from tree to tree, and from rock to rock, he was coming down a water-worn gully towards the hut. He wore no coat. His shirt and breeches were in rags. A tangle of long unkempt hair covered his head, and merged into a scrubby growth of beard on his cheeks and chin. He carried a small furry creature in his hands. His position was such that he could not see the other party, any more than the Germans could see him. Each oblivious to the other's presence, they were converging on the same spot—the ramshackle hut.

'It's him!' Biggles hissed the two vital words.

'How do you know?' breathed Thirty. 'I don't recognize him.'

'Look at his field-boots. Boots like that are only cut in England.'

'Then I'm going to save him,' said Thirty in a strangled voice, and leaping forward, opened his mouth to shout.

With a panther-like bound Biggles sprang at him

and bore him to the ground, his hand over his mouth. 'Quiet, you idiot,' he grated savagely. 'Do you want to get us all killed. We can't take on rifles with automatics at this range.' He released his grip and got up.

Thirty, crestfallen, and looking near to tears, did the same. 'This is a case of more haste less speed,' muttered Biggles. 'We can do nothing but watch—for the moment.'

Resuming their look-out positions they were in time to see the third act of the grim play that was in progress. Forty—assuming it was Forty—suddenly scrambled up the side of the gully so that he stood in a position where the hut was in plain view. Unfortunately for him, in his ascent a loose stone had become dislodged and went crashing down to the bottom of the gully, taking several others with it.

At the noise, the members of the enemy party crouched low in the gorse and heather with which the more open parts of the hill-side were covered. Forty also remained motionless for a few moments, but as nothing happened he continued his journey, now running swiftly across the open area towards the hut, unaware of the many eyes that were watching him. Reaching the hut, he disappeared from view.

Instantly the five German soldiers sprang to their feet, and, spreading out fanwise, converged swiftly on the hut. As they neared it, however, they slowed down, drawing closer to each other. Presently all five of them stood together outside the door.

With parted lips and staring eyes, his heart pounding furiously against his ribs, Thirty watched what he knew would be the next move.

The *unter offizier* made a signal to his men; their rifles

covered door and window. Then, with his own rifle ready for instant action he pushed the door open and disappeared from sight. His voice barked an order, clearly heard by the airmen. The soldiers hurried forward. They, too, disappeared into the hut, and once more the hill-side was deserted.

'This is our cue,' snapped Biggles. 'It's now or never. Come on.'

Sliding, jumping, and sometimes falling, they tore down the hill-side. Through the brook at the bottom and up the other side towards the hut they sped, panting under the strain of their exertions until they were within a dozen yards of their objective, when Biggles flung up his hand in a signal to halt. Thirty, his automatic clutched in his right hand, brushed the perspiration from his eyes with the other, and waited for the next move. It was not long in coming.

Crouching low, with the stealth of an Indian on the war-path, Biggles made his way to the rear of the hut, where he sank on to his right knee and beckoned the others to join him. From inside the hut came the harsh voice of the *unter offizier*, answered occasionally by a softer tone.

'We shall have to wait until they come out,' breathed Biggles. 'Jump out when I do and be ready to shoot like lightning. If they drop their rifles and put their hands up, all right, but any move by one of them to raise his rifle, let him have it. It's the only way. It's either they or we for it, and they won't hesitate to shoot *us*. Ssh! here they come.'

The airmen, placed as they were on the far side of the hut from the door, could not, of course, see the others; they could only guess what was happening by the sound of their voices and movements. They heard the door creak back on its hinges, the shuffle of footsteps and the soft thud of the butts of the Germans' rifles as they were rested on the ground.

Thirty could see Biggles bracing his muscles for the spring that would reveal their presence, so he was at his heels when, with the lithe agility of a panther, and his pistol held out in front of him, Biggles darted into the open.

'*Hände hoch*\*!' he snapped.

There was a moment or two of utter silence; a curious silence; a hush that was charged with expectancy, like the lull between a flash of lightning and the crash of thunder. The Germans stood still, in the positions in which the shock of surprise had found them, staring wide-eyed at the three automatics that menaced them. Then, like a film that breaks and is continued, movement was restored.

With a low snarl the *unter offizier* jerked up his rifle, but almost as soon as the movement began Biggles's pistol roared. The movement ceased, and the look of hate on the *unter offizier's* face turned to wonder. Then his legs seemed to fold up under him and he crashed to the ground like a wet overcoat falling from a peg.

Simultaneously with this, another of the Germans moved his rifle, but he desisted as Thirty's automatic jerked round to him. Another leapt backwards to the side of the hut so swiftly that he was out of sight when Algy's bullet ripped a splinter from the corner of the building.

'Get him,' ejaculated Biggles, and then counter-

---

\* German: hands up!

manded the order as the man was heard to be crashing down the hill-side. 'All right, let him go,' muttered Biggles, whose automatic had never wavered from the others. He stepped forward, and, one after the other, took the rifles out of their hands and threw them in a heap on the ground. '*Gehen*\*!' he told them, pointing in the direction from which they had come.

The Germans, pale-faced, backed away for a few yards, and then turning, they walked hurriedly away, breaking into a run as soon as they were out of effective range.

Turning, Biggles flashed a quick glance at the bearded man in the tattered clothes who, during all this time, had not moved. He appeared to be even more dazed than the Germans at the swift sequence of events. Biggles spoke briskly. 'Are you Fortymore?'

'Yes.'

'Come on, then. We'll leave the handshakes until afterwards if you don't mind. Let's get out of this. We've some way to go, and things will be pretty hot here presently.'

Without waiting for the other to reply he started off at a dog-trot down the valley. The others followed. But before they had taken a dozen steps two things happened at once. The bellow of an aero engine sent the birds wheeling into the air, and somewhere not far away a rifle cracked. The bullet struck a piece of rock just in front of Biggles and richocheted, screaming, into the air.

'It's the Hun who bolted,' yelled Biggles. 'Run for it.'

* German: Go!

Twice more the rifle cracked, the report reverberating from hill to hill, but either the German was a bad shot, or the running, crouching figures were too difficult a target, for the shots, like the first one, struck harmlessly against the hill-side.

Immediately afterwards the four airmen rounded the spur of rock which concealed them from the rest of the valley. But Biggles did not stop. Running, and jumping over obstacles, he raced on down the gorge that led to the machines, and not until they were in sight of them did he ease the pace. He slowed down for the rescued prisoner to catch up with him, for, due no doubt to the privations he had endured, Forty was catching his breath in gasps, and it was clear that he was near the end of his endurance.

'Sorry to rush you like this,' apologized Biggles, 'but after shooting that Hun we can't afford to get caught. Not much farther to go. There are our machines.'

Forty had no breath to answer. He could only nod.

A minute later they reached the machines, and it was clear from a glance that Rip had obeyed his orders to the letter. The Bristol's propeller was ticking over, and Rip was standing by the nose of Biggles's machine.

'All right, easy all,' called Biggles. 'Everything in order, Rip?'

'Not a sign of any one,' replied Rip. 'You've got him, then?' he added, grinning with delight as he looked at the new member of their party.

'We can't talk now; there will be a bunch of Huns here in a few minutes. Let's get away. Forty, you travel in the back seat of the Biff*. Thirty, you know the way

* R.F.C. nickname for Bristol Fighter.

80

I told you to go home. Go to it. Don't stop whatever happens. We must reckon that those Huns we've just left will get on the telephone and set things buzzing, so we may have to fight. Never mind if Algy and I stop; you keep going for the lines as fast as you can go. That's all.'

The party split up, each member hurrying to his allotted machine. Rip started Biggles's propeller, then Algy's, afterwards climbing up into the back seat of the Bristol in which Forty was already standing. 'Bit of a squeeze, I'm afraid,' he grinned. 'Be awkward if we have to use the gun.'

'You lie flat on the floor,' Forty told him, 'that's the best way. It will spread the weight, and give me room to work the gun if we run into a rough house.'

Further conversation was cut short by the roar of the three engines as the machines moved forward.

Thirty, after a glance to make sure that the others were ready, opened his throttle wide. The Bristol surged forward, tail up. Except for taking a longer run than usual to get off it behaved as usual, and he drew a deep breath of relief as he banked slowly round until his nose was pointing to the west. A quick look over his shoulder revealed the two Camels taking up position just above and behind him, so he resumed his course with joy and confidence in his heart.

'An hour and we'll be safe,' he thought exultantly.

# Chapter 8

# A Race for Life

But in this he was not quite correct. He was to learn what many other British pilots had already learned— sometimes to their cost—that a return journey from enemy country could take a good deal longer than the outward trip because of the wind, which in northern France almost invariably blows from west to east, retarding the speed of a plane in direct ratio to its force.

The machines had been in the air for nearly an hour when Thirty first became aware of this unfortunate factor. He was flying level at ten thousand feet when his astonished eyes fell on a conspicuous landmark, a lake, which he had noticed on the outward journey. According to his calculations, based on time, they ought to be nearly home, whereas he had a clear recollection of passing over the lake a good twenty minutes after they had crossed the lines. This meant, in effect, that they had not covered more than two-thirds of the return journey.

Looking down, he saw what he hoped to see. Smoke. There is nothing unusual in this; one can usually see smoke of some sort from the air. In this case it was being generated by a smouldering bonfire in a corner of a field, and a grunt of disgust broke from his lips. From the way the smoke rolled low over the ground he knew that the wind—which, as usual, had risen after the sun was up—could not be less than twenty-five miles an hour.

So far they had not seen a single aircraft of any sort, but now he looked around the sky anxiously, and was not a little relieved to see that it was still clear, except far away to the west, where the top of a long line of cumulus clouds was just showing, like a breaking wave, above the horizon.

The Bristol roared on towards them, as if anxious to make their acquaintance, the engine voicing its rhythmic bellow which, by reason of its very regularity, Thirty barely noticed.

He had just sat up straight after picking up his map, which had fallen to the floor, when, with a start, he saw Biggles's Camel surge down beside him. He saw that Biggles was pointing, urging him to a slightly more southerly course. He complied at once, but, naturally, wondered why Biggles had taken this step. The other Camel returned to its original position, so he stared hard down the course he would have followed had not the change been made. For some time he could see nothing unusual, but then he caught his breath sharply as his eyes fell on a number of tiny objects that were moving across the landscape. But for the fact that they were in perfect V formation they might have been insects, so small were they; and they might, literally, have been crawling on the ground, which is the invariable effect created in such circumstances. They were still too far away for Thirty to make out their national markings, or recognize the type, but he knew that they could only be enemy machines so far over the lines.

Watching them closely, he saw that they were flying

on a straight course that would soon take them out of sight, but as he regarded them apprehensively he saw the light flash on the top plane of the leader, and he knew that he had turned. One by one the other machines of the formation followed, a brilliant streak of light flashing for an instant from each one in turn as the rays of the sun caught the polished wing surfaces.

Continuing to watch, now with marked apprehension, Thirty saw that the formation had altered its course and was now standing directly towards them. The inference was obvious. They had been seen by the lynx-eyed leader of the enemy patrol, who was coming to investigate. A minute later Thirty could see the black crosses on their wing-tips; and, as before, they gave him a queer thrill. He realized now that the ever-vigilant Biggles had spotted the enemy machines the instant they had come within his range of vision, and the change of course he had ordered was an attempt to escape observation.

Thirty stared ahead fixedly through his centre-section hoping to see the lines, for the question seemed to him to be one of whether the enemy machines would overtake them, and climb up to them, before they reached the security of their own country.

Five minutes passed slowly. Thirty, glancing at his watch every few seconds, found it difficult to believe that it was only five minutes, that time could move so slowly.

Looking back at the enemy machines he saw that they were now no more than a thousand feet below, and perhaps a quarter of a mile behind. Still in formation, they were banking very slowly to a course that would bring them immediately behind the three British machines.

Thirty looked over his shoulder to make sure that his brother had seen them; there was no need to ask; Forty was leaning idly against the rear gun mounting, staring down at the enemy scouts with an expression of bored indifference. The sight did a lot to restore Thirty's confidence, and he looked back again at the enemy. He could only see three of them now, for the others were immediately behind him; he recognized them for Albatros scouts, and saw that they were creeping up steadily.

Raising his eyes he saw that the Camels were still just above and behind him. This rather surprised him, for he rather expected that they would have done something, although what, he did not know. Still, it did not occur to him to question Biggles's judgement.

Looking at his watch for the hundredth time he saw that they had been in the air for an hour and a quarter, and a glance ahead still revealed no sign of the lines. What it did reveal, however, was a mighty mass of cloud, four or five thousand feet thick, rolling towards them, and not more than two or three miles away. He hoped that Biggles would give him a lead as to whether he should remain above it or go under it, and he was still staring at it when from a yawning blue chasm in the centre of it there burst five scarlet-painted Triplanes*. He stared at them in unspeakable horror, for from their actions it was instantly clear that the enemy machines had seen those bearing the red, white, and blue rings. The Triplanes were between them and the

* German fighter with three wings, with two forward firing guns. Also called by the slang name of tripehounds.

lines. Thirty's heart sank. 'We're cut off; they've got us between two fires,' he thought bitterly.

Looking up behind him he saw that Biggles and Algy had closed up; they were signalling to each other with swift gesticulations, a ridiculous-looking dumb panto-mime. Evidently they understood each other, for Algy nodded assent. Almost at once the nose of his Camel tilted downwards and Biggles forged past the Bristol in a steep dive, beckoning to Thirty to follow him.

Thirty obeyed without hesitation, regardless of the fact that the three machines, with the two Camels leading, were roaring straight towards the five Tri-planes, which, being slightly below them, had tilted up their noses to meet them.

To Thirty, the next few seconds were the acme of breathless excitement. As straight as a hawk swooping on its prey, Biggles's machine plunged towards the red formation. Thirty, being behind, saw everything. His heart seemed to stop beating, as, with a sort of spell-bound fascination, he waited for what appeared to be a wholesale collision. Something told him that whatever happened Biggles would not turn. A curious feeling of finality stole over him, leaving him strangely calm. He would not turn, either, he decided. So, tight-lipped, he waited for the crash. He saw little jabs of flame start dancing at the muzzles of the guns on the crimson cowlings; saw the swift streak of tracer bullets spurt from the nose of Biggles's machine. Perhaps two hundred yards separated the two formations, and they were still hurtling straight to destruction.

He had braced himself for the shock of the head-on collision when the German formation split like a covey of partridges driven over guns, some zooming to the right, others to the left. His left wing-tip missed a red one by perhaps ten feet. He could see every detail of it, the tappits working in the engine and the faint smoke trail of the exhaust. He saw the pilot's face clearly, the fixed stare in his eyes behind the goggles, and the set mouth. He heard a gun behind him stutter for an instant. Then the two machines swept past each other. The air ahead was clear.

Immediately Biggles steepened his dive to such a degree that Thirty used both hands on the joystick to keep pace with him. He became conscious of a great noise in his ears, a kind of wailing scream that rose to a shrill crescendo. He risked a glance behind. The sky seemed to be full of machines. He had no time to see more, for it needed all his skill to keep close to the two Camels, which, swerving, had plunged into the aerial chasm between the cloud masses from which the Tri-planes had appeared.

Even at that desperate moment he found time to marvel on it, for it was a scene such as not even Dante could have imagined. It was unreal; a fantasy. Below lay a colossal pit, the base of which was lost in blue mist. On either side, ice-blue walls towered up to the paler blue of heaven. Billows of gleaming white, so bright that they dazzled the eyes, flecked the sun-drenched rim of this stupendous cavity, the bottom and sides of which were as intangible as the atmosphere through which they roared. The noise of the engines took on a strange muffled note.

Down—down—down they plunged, sometimes swerving round little islands of pale grey mist that floated in the void, dispersing others as they burst through them. Again Thirty heard the gun behind him, and snatching a glance over his shoulder saw Forty shooting at something which the tail of the machine prevented him from seeing.

Biggles turned sharply to the right, so sharply that the Bristol overshot him. Recovering quickly, however, Thirty followed, and now being broadside to his original course saw clearly what had before been hidden from his view. Roaring down the misty gorge were nearly a score of machines. It was an amazing sight, one that printed itself indelibly on his memory.

A large, dark-green two-seater, with the tell-tale black crosses on its wings and fuselage, suddenly came into view at the far end of the gorge, evidently with the idea of using the passage to get above the clouds. The speed with which it turned and plunged blindly into the wall of cloud brought a faint smile to Thirty's lips. Then, suddenly, he saw the ground, dim with the shadow of the great cloud mass that hung over it like a pall. A little way ahead it changed from dull green to brown. Thirty recognized the lines. At the same moment Biggles and Algy both turned outwards, allowing him to pass between them. He would have turned, too, but Biggles signalled to him to go on, and an instant later they had passed out of his field of view. He knew what they had done. They had turned to meet the enemy machines, which, being single-seaters, had drawn so close to the two-seater that it would have been fatal to go on. Alone, doubtless they could have given the enemy the slip, but they could not—or rather, would not—leave the slower two-seater.

Thirty looked at his altimeter. The needle was just below the two-thousand mark, so much height had they lost in their rush through the hole in the clouds. He looked back, trying to find it, hoping to see the two Camels emerge; but either it had closed up or there was nothing to indicate where it was. He was still looking when a smart blow on the head made him turn. Forty pointed. Following the line indicated, Thirty's heart gave a lurch when he saw four machines almost on top of him. He breathed again when he recognized them for Camels, but it gave him a jolt to realize that although they were so close he had not seen them until they had been pointed out to him. Almost at once he saw that they were from his own squadron, Mahoney's red, yellow, and blue streamers conspicuous in the lead.

An idea came into his head. Flying close, he beckoned, and then turned back towards the clouds. Another shock awaited him as his nose came round, for the sky through which he had flown was black with archie bursts. Somehow it didn't worry him. He felt that the four Camels ought to know where Biggles and Algy were. But it was in vain that he searched for the cavity through which he had just come.

He jumped, literally, when, without warning, a red Triplane fell out of the cloud and plunged across his nose, the rear part smothered in a sheet of flame. He saw the luckless pilot trying to get out. Then it passed out of sight below him. An Albatros shot out of the cloud, but as quickly disappeared into it again when, apparently, the pilot saw the four Camels. Another Triplane came out, gliding, with a dead propeller; a Camel shot out a little way beyond it. The Triplane went into a spin, and the Camel started circling. From the fact that it carried no streamers Thirty knew it must be Algy.

Biggles came out of the cloud a good deal higher up;

he, too, circled for a moment and then came down to join the others, but swerved away towards the lines before reaching them. Thirty followed, after noting that the other Camels were turning to do the same.

The nose of Biggles's Camel went down, and the seven machines scattered and, in no sort of formation, dived through the ever-present archie across the shell-torn strip of no-man's-land.

'We're home,' Thirty told himself unbelievingly.

He landed near Algy's machine. Algy came running over to him, laughing almost hysterically.

'My gosh! Did you see that old Hun two-seater scuttle when he saw us?' he chuckled.

'Yes,' answered Thirty, lamely, wondering how Algy could laugh. He himself felt oddly weak. His mouth was dry, and the skin seemed to be tightly drawn over his face. Stiffly, he climbed out on to the wing and jumped to the ground.

# Chapter 9
# Forty Makes a Proposition

Forty also climbed down, followed by Rip, looking not a little relieved to vacate his cramped position. Mahoney joined them, and in a few minutes they were all laughing and joking.

'Lucky you arrived at such a useful moment,' Thirty told Mahoney.

'Lucky? I wouldn't call it luck,' replied the flight-commander. 'Biggles asked me to hang about in case you ran into trouble.'

'I thought we might be glad of Mahoney's help if we finished up with a rush—as indeed we did,' said Biggles. 'Here comes the C.O. You'd better leave the explaining to me; he'd be in order in ticking us off; in fact, I think he will.'

Major Mullen joined the party, his face expressing his astonishment when he saw Forty. 'Who is this fellow?' he asked, stiffly.

'Fortymore, sir, of eighty-four squadron,' answered Biggles.

'*What?*'

'He was shot down some time ago, sir, and made prisoner. He had a sort of an arrangement with his brother—that is, Fortymore of our squadron—as to where he would make for if he got clear of the Huns. We went over to-day and picked him up. That's all, sir.' Such was Biggles's account of the adventures of the morning.

Major Mullen addressed Forty. 'Do you mean to say—you've just come out of—*Germany*?' he asked incredulously.

'Yes, sir.'

The C.O. looked from one to the other. 'Great Heaven,' he said softly. He thought for a moment. 'You'd better go and have a bath and some food and get into some decent clothes,' he told Forty, at last. 'I shall have to report this to Wing* at once. Come up to the squadron office as soon as you are ready. You'd better come too,' he added, looking at Biggles and Thirty in turn. 'Hurry up; I expect Major Raymond will want a word with you.' With that he turned and walked towards his office.

'Who's Major Raymond?' Thirty asked Biggles.

'Wing Intelligence Officer. I should say he will come over; he doesn't get a chance to interview some one straight out of Germany every day. Come on, Forty; let's find you some togs.'

Biggles was right in his assumption that Major Raymond would want to interview Forty and hear at first-hand the details of the exploit, for when those who had been ordered to do so gathered at the squadron office about an hour later he was already there. He looked at Forty—now shaved, and spick and span in a borrowed uniform—for several seconds before congratulating him on his escape.

'Surely you are the officer who put forward such a scheme some time ago?' he remarked.

* The administrative headquarters. Each Wing commanded several squadrons. It was headed by a Lieutenant-Colonel.

'That is correct, sir. I did, but it came to nothing. It's queer that I should have been able to prove it in actual practice; naturally, although I spoke about it, I hardly expected it to come off. Even now it hardly seems possible. Less than three hours ago I was in Germany, and had been run to earth in my hiding-place by an armed guard.'

Thereafter, for the benefit of the C.O. and the Wing officer, the whole story was related from the beginning, omitting, of course, all reference to Thirty and Rip's irregular arrival in France, which was something Forty himself did not yet know, since with being occupied by an extensive toilet and a square meal, Thirty had not had time to tell him. In any case, he was wondering if he ought to do so, since his brother was a senior officer.

When the story had ended, Major Raymond tossed the end of his cigarette through the open window. 'Well, that's the most astonishing tale I've heard since I came to France,' he observed slowly.

Thirty found himself wondering what the major would think if he knew the *whole* truth of his escapade.

'What had I better do, sir? Report back to my squadron?' asked Forty.

'No, you can't do that,' replied the major quietly.

'Why not, sir?'

'What I meant was, you can never fly over the lines again.'

Forty's face showed his consternation.

'You know the rules of war,' went on the major, 'or you ought to. If an escaped prisoner is ever retaken by the enemy he can be shot, since he comes into the category of a spy. If you made a strong application to go on flying there is always a chance, of course, that the higher authority would allow you to do so, but your blood would be on your own head—so to speak. That has happened in the one or two rare cases of an officer getting out of Germany, but if he was captured in France, he is sent to another theatre of war—Palestine or East Africa, for instance. But to tell you the truth, what I cannot help feeling is this: if this can be done once it should be possible to do it again. Officers of experience are very valuable just now, and there are hundreds in German prison camps.'

'I don't see how it could be done again, sir,' said Biggles. 'You must remember that this was an exceptional case in that a landing-ground—or, shall we say, a picking-up ground—had been more or less pre-arranged. I'm not saying we couldn't land, but it would be no use landing if the fellows in the prison camps did not know where to make for.'

'It might be arranged for the future, though,' observed the major reflectively. 'A number of rendez-vous could be pin-pointed, and officers made acquainted with them, so that if they were shot down they would know where to make for. I take it that you were actually captured by the enemy, Fortymore?'

'Oh, yes, sir. Not immediately, though. I was on the run for a time. Then I was caught and sent to Tatzgart. I got away with several other fellows the very next day, and there I was lucky, for they had a tunnel which they had been digging for three months. By mutual consent we agreed to separate after we got out so as not to attract attention. Naturally, I made straight for Berglaken, although with a good deal more hope than confidence that my brother would come over for me.'

'It is a pity there is no way of letting the fellows in

prison camps know . . . but there, I do not think we need pursue that.'

'My original plan, you remember, sir, was not only to pick fellows up, but to establish food dumps, with maps, wire-cutters, rubber gloves for getting through electrified wire, and so on, so that they would at least stand a good chance of getting across the frontier even if they were not picked up,' explained Forty.

'Well, I certainly think it's worth going into,' declared Major Raymond. 'I'll see what headquarters have to say about it. We should need volunteers to run such a show, of course. It would be a lot too risky to *order* fellows to do it.'

'Well, you wouldn't have to look very far, sir,' put in Biggles.

A faint smile crossed the major's face as he looked at Biggles. 'Trust you to be in it,' he said lightly.

'I didn't do so badly this time, sir,' Biggles reminded him.

'Well, we'll see,' went on the major. 'There would be a big risk in letting the information be generally known over this side of the line—and we should have to do that to make the thing possible—as a spy might get hold of it. Once it got back to Germany it would be all up. The Huns would simply set a trap at the rendezvous and catch the rescue pilots red-handed. Still, I'll think about that.'

'Pardon me, sir,' put in Forty. 'You said just now that there was no possible way of letting fellows already in prison camps know.'

The major raised his eyebrows. 'Can you think of a way?'

'Yes, sir.'

'Well?'

'I could go back.'

Dead silence followed the words. It was as if every one were trying to work out just what Forty meant.

'Go *back*?' said the major.

'Exactly, sir. In other words, I could be dumped back over the lines—and get myself recaptured. I should be put back into prison. I would then pass the necessary information to fellows whom I knew.'

The major stared at Forty as if he could not believe his ears. 'Good heavens!' he gasped. 'Are you serious?'

'Quite serious, sir.'

'Don't do it,' burst out Thirty impulsively. 'Why, they'll shoot you the moment they retake you.'

'Why should they?' asked Forty naïvely. 'They would hardly be likely to recognize me. On the only occasion that they saw me I looked pretty dishevelled and wore R.N.A.S.* blue uniform. I could arrange to go down a hundred miles farther north than last time. Shaven, in R.F.C. uniform, and with a name like—say—John Smithson, there seems to me to be no earthly reason why they should associate me with the R.N.A.S. officer by the name of Fortymore who escaped from Tatzgart.'

'By jove! That's true enough,' cried Major Raymond. 'What do you think, Mullen?'

'I agree with Fortymore; there should be little or no danger of recognition; all the same, I believe the German prison camps are stiff with counter-espionage agents, so there are bound to be risks.'

'Yes, I think it's too risky,' declared Thirty emphatically.

* Royal Naval Air Service

'If by this scheme we can serve more usefully than as ordinary flying members of a squadron, I think it's up to us to do it,' said Forty, simply. 'And I've one or two pals in Boche prisons; nothing would give me greater personal satisfaction than to get them away.'

'We've all got one or two there, if it comes to that,' murmured Biggles.

Major Raymond rose and picked up his cap. 'I must be getting along,' he said quietly, looking at his wristwatch. 'If you fellows hear no more about this you will know it is a washout, and I'll arrange for you, Fortymore, to be sent home for a spot of leave. Otherwise I'll call another conference. I hope you won't object to my borrowing your officers, Mullen, if we do decide to do something about it.'

The C.O. of 266 squadron made a wry face. 'Naturally, I shouldn't be pleased about it,' he returned, and then sighed. 'But, as we say, there is a war on, so I suppose we shall all have to put our backs into it.'

Major Raymond shook hands with Forty. 'Goodbye,' he said. 'And, once more, good show. Goodbye, gentlemen.'

'That's all,' Major Mullen told his officers, briefly. 'Wash out for the rest of the day.'

# Chapter 10

# A Dangerous Mission

A week had elapsed since Forty had made his daring and courageous offer to Major Raymond. The period had been one of expectancy, and, to some extent, anxiety. Three days after the conversation in the squadron office, Major Raymond had called another meeting, at which he had reported the decision of the higher command to permit the 'Rescue Flight'—as it was now called—to be formed; and, in accordance with this decision, he had invited Forty and Biggles to put their heads together and submit to him a plan of the suggested procedure.

This they had done, Thirty, Rip, Algy, and Mahoney attending the discussion. The scheme which had been evolved was simple. With the assistance of the map, and one or two risky excursions over Germany, three lonely areas where landings could be made had been selected. These were some distance from each other, and had been labelled aerodromes A, B, and C. Landings had actually been made at these places to confirm their suitability, the time chosen—as on the occasion when they had rescued Forty—being the break of dawn.

A provisional rescue flight had been formed consisting of Biggles, Algy, Thirty, and Rip. Mahoney was not included, although to his flight had been allocated the duty of flying out to meet returning machines and escorting them home.

Forty, flying under an assumed name, was to allow himself to be recaptured. In the prison camp he was to tell officers whom he could trust implicitly the position of the landing-grounds. Thus, should they succeed in getting out of the prison camps they could make for the nearest one with a fair hope of being picked up in a short time, since the rescue flight was to visit each landing-ground once a week. In the interval of waiting, the escapees would be able to live on food which would be *cached** in the northern ditch, or hedge, of the landing-ground by the rescue flight when they landed. An escaped officer arriving at one of the landing-grounds was to signify his presence by leaving a piece of newspaper somewhere on the outskirts of the field; to a passer-by, it would be no more than a piece of waste paper. This would prevent the rescue flight making an unnecessary landing.

In view of the success of the previous raid it was decided to use the same machines. Only the Bristol would land, the two Camels acting as look-outs while the Bristol was on the ground, and as an escort when it was in the air.

The greatest risk of the whole thing, apart from a bad landing, which would, of course, leave Rip and Thirty on the ground on the wrong side of the lines, was that one of the enemy agents who were known to frequent the prison camps might hear of the plan and cause a trap to be set. These particular agents were selected on account of their knowledge of the English

* Hidden

99

language; dressed as British officers, and mingling with them even to the extent of sharing their privations, it was almost impossible to detect them. This was the reason why Forty had decided only to impart the secret to officers whom he recognized, or to officers for whom *they* could vouch. Nevertheless, there was always a chance that one of those in the know might, in an unguarded moment, let slip a few words which would be pounced upon by the agents whose duty it was to listen for such remarks.

To this arrangement Major Raymond had added only one suggestion, or rather, request. He asked Forty to memorize a list of names of officers who, for some reason known only to themselves, the higher command were particularly anxious to recover. The whereabouts of these particular officers had been made known to the British authorities by their agents in Germany. Naturally, Forty would only be able to communicate with those in whose camp he found himself. That was all, except that Forty was at liberty to come out of Germany, getting himself picked up by the rescue flight, if and when he had reason to suppose that he was under suspicion.

This settled, the rest of the time had been spent by the members of the special flight making themselves word-perfect in the arrangements and overhauling the machines. And now, on a bright summer's morning, the first move was to be made to put the plan into operation. Forty had to smash his machine deliberately, but as naturally as possible, on the wrong side of the lines. Their goodbyes having been said, they sat in their machines and waited for Biggles, who was having a last word from his cockpit with the C.O. Although on this occasion, since they would not have to make a landing, there was no reason why Thirty and Rip should not fly their Camels, they had chosen to use the Bristol so as to become thoroughly proficient in the handling of it. In front of their own hangar the propellers of Mahoney's machines were also ticking over, for they were to follow the leading formation and support it should it be attacked by a large number of enemy scouts—which might result in a disaster at the very onset of the operations. A few minutes later the eight machines were in the air, the Bristol in front, with its escort of three Camels giving it the appearance of a photographic machine, and Mahoney's flight some two thousand feet above and behind. These positions were maintained as they roared through the usual barrage of archie over the lines into the enemy sky.

It was twenty minutes before they saw a hostile machine, and then it was only an old Rumpler* which veered off when it saw them coming. Biggles made no attempt to follow it; with his mind concentrated on the major issue he had no inclination to bother about stray machines. So he turned north-west and set off on a new course parallel with the trenches.

Within a few minutes he saw what he had been hoping to find: a small formation of enemy scouts; five Albatroses in loose formation. They were heading east, apparently returning from a patrol. Biggles turned slightly to cut them off, and his nose went down for the necessary speed.

It was no doubt due to the fact that they were some way from the lines that the leader of the German patrol

---

* German two-seater biplane for observation and light bombing raids.

101

was not keeping a very keen look-out. Or it may have been that, feeling secure, he had relaxed his vigilance. Be that as it may, the Camels were within range before they were seen, and the result, as often happened in such cases, was instant confusion, each Albatros pilot acting as he thought best. Two of them collided. It was not a violent collision; their wing-tips merely brushed, but for one it was sufficient. His wing crumpled and he went down, spinning. The other cut his engine and also started going down, but under control. Of the other three, one dived out of the fight. The other two turned, but finding themselves outnumbered, broke off after firing a few shots and dived for home. It was a brief affair, and just such a one as Biggles had hoped for.

Thirty paid little attention to the Germans. He was watching Forty, for a dog-fight was his cue to depart on his dangerous mission. He saw Forty look at him, and his hand go up in a signal of farewell. Biting his lip, Thirty waved back. The propeller of Forty's Camel slowed; a wing-tip dropped; the nose followed, and, the next moment the machine was spinning earthward.

Thirty continued to circle, watching the spinning machine, terrified lest make-believe should become reality, and it failed to come out. But a few hundred feet above the ground it levelled out and went into a shallow dive, rocking as if it were not completely under control. There was no field large enough for it to land in, but Forty, playing his part, acted as though he had no choice but to land. He attempted to side-slip into the largest field. The wheels touched. But there was no distance between it and the boundary, and a moment later it had plunged into the hedge.

Still watching, Thirty saw Forty climb out; saw his Very pistol* flash. A tongue of flame appeared near the tank. The next moment Forty ran clear as flames enveloped the whole machine. Other figures appeared, running towards the fire.

After that Thirty's attention was attracted by Biggles flying across his nose, beckoning to him to follow; which he did, realizing that by holding up the others so far from the lines he was endangering their lives. So after a last quick look at the blazing machine on the ground—which Forty had, of course, fired to prevent it from falling into the hands of the enemy—and the lonely figure standing in the field, he turned and followed his flight-commander.

They reached the lines without incident; which was just as well, for Thirty was preoccupied with his thoughts, and had they been attacked he might have come badly out of the fight. It was only natural that he should have dreaded this moment; he had been steeling himself for it for days, but now the time had come his intense anxiety could not be allayed. He had visions of Forty being interrogated by hard-faced Prussians; of the sinister wall of evil repute behind the riding-school at Lille, where agents met their fate, alone, in the cold grey of dawn.

Thrusting these dismal thoughts aside with an effort he discovered that the Camels were below him, gliding down. He saw the aerodrome, and, presently, landed on it himself.

'Well, that all went off like clockwork,' said Biggles,

* Short-barrelled pistol for firing coloured flares, used as a signal. Before the days of radio in aircraft different coloured flares were often used to pass messages.

joining him. Then, noticing Thirty's depressed expression, 'Don't worry; he'll be all right,' he added comfortingly. 'We shall see him again shortly.'

'I wish I was as sure of that as you seem to be,' answered Thirty, a trifle bitterly. 'And "shortly" you say. A fortnight at the very least. Anything can happen in that time.'

'Well, we couldn't make it any less,' murmured Biggles, with a slight shrug. 'We've got to give Forty time to get the thing going—divulge the plan to the right people; and then they've got to get away. We arranged that it should be a fortnight before we made our first patrol; but, personally, I think we shall be lucky if we find any one waiting. These prison camps are not so easy to get out of as all that.'

Thirty nodded. 'Well, I suppose we can only wait and see,' he observed philosophically; and then, turning, he made his way slowly to his room.

# Chapter 11
# Rescue Flight to the Rescue

There is an old saying, and a true one, that all things come to an end. Nevertheless, before the arranged fourteen days had expired Thirty was beginning seriously to doubt it. Never had time seemed so long. There was little he could do except make himself thoroughly proficient with the Bristol by flying it in all weathers and making innumerable practice forced landings, for the C.O. had ruled that the rescue flight—as the special flight was now unofficially called—was not to go over the lines on ordinary duties unless enemy activity made it imperative, his reason being the justifiable fear that a casualty would upset the entire scheme, with possibly disastrous results for those officers who, having taken desperate risks to get out of prison, might wait in vain to be picked up.

But the last day of the period of waiting had come and gone, and two hours before dawn the following morning the members of the rescue flight were assembled on the tarmac having a final word before making their first raid into enemy territory.

'We proceed straight to aerodrome A,' Biggles was saying. 'If there is no indication that any one is waiting on the ground we come straight back. It would be asking for trouble to go on to aerodrome B in broad daylight. If we see a piece of paper on the field, you go down and land, Thirty. As soon as you are down, taxi up to the northern boundary, where Rip will jump down and dump the food parcel in the hedge; afterwards returning at the double to the machine. That's all—except that if no one shows up you take straight off again. Obviously, if any one is there he'll be on the look-out; if he isn't, well, it's his own fault. We daren't risk waiting. Any one any questions to ask?'

Receiving no answer, Biggles turned to his machine. 'All right, then,' he said. 'Let's get away.'

In a few minutes the formation, comprising, as before, two Camels and a Bristol Fighter, were climbing towards the lines and their distant objective. Having already flown over the ground, and as visibility was good, they were able to ignore their compasses and fly by landmarks, an almost full moon—which Biggles had taken into consideration when making his plans— making the major physical features of the ground underneath as clear as though it were daylight.

There was the usual business of signalling to the British searchlight and archie batteries, and dodging those on the German side, and then the three machines roared on through the deserted hostile sky, the two Camels marking the Bristol by the glow of its exhaust*.

As a matter of detail the sky was not altogether

* In the air, the glow of an exhaust is much more apparent than those who have never flown by night might expect. In daylight the exhaust pipe of a stationary engine does not appear to change colour, but by night it glows red, for it becomes, in fact, red-hot. From it the exhausted gas pours like a streak of fire, which, appearing to be much too close to the fuselage for safety, has scared many a pilot making his first flight by night. This glow is, of course, visible to another machine close to it in the air, but it can seldom be seen from the ground, owing both to the altitude of the machine and the fact that, in the case of anything but a high-wing monoplane, it is shielded by the lower wings. Both the Bristol Fighter and the Camel were biplanes.

deserted, as Thirty, to his alarm, presently discovered when a vague shape loomed up suddenly in front of him. It was so entirely unexpected that he stared at it for a full second, wondering what it could be. Then, instinctively, he kicked his rudder-bar, and swerved wildly, just as the approaching object zoomed upward. For a split second he had a glimpse of undercarriage wheels and spreading wings from which protruded a blunt-nosed nacelle; above it rose the bulky, leather-clad figure of the observer, clinging to his gun as he stared at the machine with which his own had so nearly collided.

Thirty recognized the type for a British F.E.* night-bomber, which must have been returning from an unknown mission; it awakened him to the knowledge that other machines were pursuing their sinister purposes through the war-skies of central Europe, and he resolved to profit by experience and keep a sharp look-out in the future.

He passed over a harp-shaped wood, and it told him that he was about half-way to his objective. Soon afterwards the stars began to fade, and the moon to lose its brilliancy, as the horizon ahead of him began slowly to pale to the soft misty grey that heralds the approach of the true dawn. Although Thirty wore silk gloves under his fur-lined leather gauntlets his hands were cold, so he beat them in turn on his knees to restore some warmth to them; he also took a piece of chocolate from the pigeon-hole in his dashboard, and munched it with satisfaction. Looking round, he

* Two-seater biplane night bomber with the engine behind the pilot, the gunner just in front of the pilot. Commonly known as a Fee in the R.F.C.

discovered that he could see the Camels clearly, for, now that the darkness had turned to a dim twilight, they had closed up and were flying at his wing-tips. Rip was leaning on his Scarf ring*.

Thirty examined the surrounding sky, above and below, but as far as he could discover there was not another machine in sight. He glanced at his watch and noted the time. 'Good,' he thought. 'Another ten minutes and we shall be there.'

As before, it was Biggles who gave the signal to lose height; and they had a lot to lose, for they had been flying at fourteen thousand feet. He surged up alongside the Bristol, and having succeeded in catching Thirty's eye, pointed downward. A moment afterwards his Camel began to sink earthward like a plate going to the bottom of a pool, the illusion of direct drop being caused by the apparent absence of forward speed due to the great height at which they were flying.

Thirty followed, every nerve alert now that the time for action had come. He stared hard at the landing-ground, or rather the place where he knew it to be, for it was still some distance ahead; he could see nothing on the ground clearly, for, as not infrequently happens, a sort of slight haze had developed and spread like a veil across the still twilight landscape.

On and on they glided, moving almost silently through the still air which, after the rarefied atmosphere above, seemed to have an almost fluid density. Still keeping together, the three machines dropped slowly through the belt of mist, and, suddenly, from

* The gun-mounting which completely encircled the gunner's cockpit. Round this ring the gun could slide to point in any direction.

just over a thousand feet, everything on the ground was plain to see.

Thirty saw at once that they had come down almost immediately over the landing-ground, and he examined it expectantly, looking for the paper signal that would mean that some one was there; or, conversely, the absence of it that would make a landing unnecessary.

From such a low height a piece of white paper could hardly be overlooked. It was there; Thirty saw it at once, a tiny white mark on the grass not far from the hedge on the northern side of the field. But the paper was not the only thing that Thirty saw: a movement a little to one side attracted his attention, and he focused his eyes on it with misgivings, and then dismay.

It was not at first easy to see what was happening. Certainly something was going on, but the parties to it were broken up into a number of separate units, although they seemed to be working to a common end. The scene, as a whole, was confused, but as he stared at it Thirty slowly realized that a hunt, or a pursuit, was in progress; it was concentrated on a wood, or rather a long belt of trees, which bounded the eastern and part of the northern sides of the unofficial landing-ground.

Down the southern extremity of this wood a man in civilian clothes was running with two dogs of the bloodhound type; or perhaps it would be more accurate to say that the two hounds were running with a man, for judging by the way he hung back on their leads he was clearly having difficulty in restraining them. Behind this trio, some ten or twelve grey-uniformed soldiers were strung out in twos and threes, all running in the same direction; that is to say, they were following the hounds. On the northern side of the wood, in the open area facing it, a number of soldiers were posted at intervals, like sentries, their rifles at the ready. From time to time small groups of soldiers burst out of the trees and then disappeared again within them. In the near distance still more soldiers were hurrying towards the scene, including a number of mounted men who were riding at a gallop. Several cars were racing down a road about a mile away.

From their actions, and their upturned faces, Thirty knew that the appearance of the aircraft had not passed unobserved. He also had reason to suspect that some of the troops were shooting at them, although none of the bullets struck his machine. More than one of the men pointed upwards, slowing down in their stride as if undecided what action to take.

Thirty observed all this in one long penetrating look, which occupied much less time than it takes to tell. And the knowledge burst upon him that if these soldiers were pursuing somebody, and it was clear that they were, it could hardly be a coincidence that the pursuit was heading towards the landing-ground—had almost reached it, in fact.

This completely unexpected situation, which was something for which no allowance had been made, threw his brain into a whirl. What ought he to do? What would Biggles expect him to do?

His decision, not unnaturally, was to open his engine and remove himself from such a dangerous vicinity with all possible speed. He did, in fact, open his throttle, but simultaneously Biggles's machine roared down past him, heading for the wood, with Biggles gesticulating violently towards the landing-ground. Algy was at

Biggles's wing-tip. Thirty saw the tracer streaming from their guns; saw some of the men on the ground dive for the cover of the trees. One fell. Close behind him Rip's gun started its harsh rattle. And still he could not make up his mind what to do. What had Biggles meant?

He looked again at the landing-ground, and caught his breath as the dark figure of a man burst from the bushes near the wood, and, ducking low, raced down the hedge. For some distance he ran as only a hunted man will run. Then he swerved out into the field and flung up both arms with a gesture of appeal that was unmistakable.

By this time Thirty had cut his engine and was going down in a steep side-slip; the gun behind him had stopped. A lightning glance over his shoulder showed him that Rip had seen the solitary man. Rip saw Thirty turn, and, bending over, he yelled in his ear, 'He's the chap they're after; we must get him.'

Thirty moistened his lips and flattened out for the landing, by no means certain of the direction of the wind. There could not be much or he would have noticed it, he thought desperately. He would have to risk it.

A bullet smashing against his engine-cowling brought forcibly to his notice the fact that he was running other risks besides a bad landing, but he set his teeth and endeavoured to remain cool in circumstances which were calculated to upset even the steadiest pilot, doing his best to touch his wheels in such a position that the Bristol would finish its run near the fugitive, who was now darting this way and that in an attempt to anticipate the stopping-place of the machine.

In the circumstances Thirty's effort was a creditable one; he kept his line fairly well, but he knew from the behaviour of the machine that he was slightly cross-wind, and he flinched as the undercarriage groaned a protest.

The Bristol never entirely stopped. The moment it began to slow down the fugitive raced madly towards it, with Rip yelling encouragement. Above the noises made by these operations came the irregular crackle of musketry, the persistent *taca-taca-taca-taca* of machine-guns from overhead, and the crash of exploding bombs.

Thirty, risking an upward glance, saw the two Camels circling and swooping low over the edge of the wood, like a pair of plovers when a dog approaches their nest. Their manoeuvring told him that Biggles and Algy were using their twenty-pound Cooper bombs, of which each carried eight, as well as their machine-guns in an attempt to hold up the pursuit. He had no time to dwell on the spectacle; grey-coated figures burst through the hedge, and bullets cut up the turf round the feet of the running fugitive who by this time had nearly reached the machine.

'Come on!' yelled Rip, although it was obvious that the man for whom they were waiting was making every effort.

Thirty, left hand ready on the throttle, felt a wave of compassion surge through him. The filthy mud-stained clothes, the ashen face, staring dark-rimmed eyes, and parted lips told their own story of dreadful ordeal. For the rest, he was a middle-aged man, with dark hair and heavy features. It was clear from his gasping breaths and distorted features that he was near the end of his endurance.

112

He got one foot into the fuselage stirrup and grabbed the edge of Rip's cockpit, but he had not the strength left to pull himself up. Rip grabbed him under the arms and dragged him in head first.

The engine roared as Thirty opened the throttle, using joystick and rudder-bar to drag the machine round to face the open field again, but even so it took some seconds to get into position for a safe take-off.

It was a frantic moment in which Thirty acted more from impulse and habit than by lucid thought, for bullets were now hitting the machine, ripping through woodwork and fabric with the terrifying force of deadly power such missiles have.

The Bristol ran forward, its speed increasing at every instant. The tail lifted. Thirty sat rigid in his seat, eyes fixed on the mark he had chosen on the far side of the field to help to keep him straight. The wheels bumped once or twice, and then the machine was off, swerving from side to side as he kicked the rudder-bar to spoil the aim of the Germans who he knew without looking were still shooting at him.

Not until the machine was at a thousand feet, sweeping round in a wide, gently climbing turn, did he dare to look around. A glance behind showed Rip standing in his cockpit emptying his drum of ammunition into the wood. The Camels had broken off and were following him, rapidly overtaking him by reason of their superior speed. 'Phew! Thank goodness,' he muttered to himself, hardly daring to believe that they had escaped without a casualty.

The Camels drew level with him and he settled down for the return journey, scanning the sky ahead with no small anxiety. But his fears proved groundless. Once he saw a small formation of enemy scouts in the distance heading towards the lines, but either the leader did not see them or he was disinclined to fight, for he made no move towards them; he also saw an enemy two-seater, several thousand feet above them, apparently returning from a reconnaissance flight over the trenches. That was all, and he breathed his satisfaction when, without having fired a shot himself, and escorted by Mahoney's flight which had come to meet them, they roared across the wilderness of no-man's-land into their own territory.

Biggles was down first, closely followed by Algy. Standing beside their machines they waited for Thirty to land and taxi in, and then hurried over to him.

'Good show,' called Biggles cheerfully, as Thirty climbed down. 'Where's the passenger?'

Rip dismounted, followed by the man they had picked up. They all waited for him to speak, but 'Thanks' was all he said and then started to walk towards the aerodrome buildings.

Algy stared at Biggles blankly. 'By gosh! Not exactly what you might call bubbling over with gratitude, is he?'

Biggles, with a curious expression on his face, hurried after the ex-fugitive. 'Hi, just a minute,' he said curtly. 'Who are you?'

A ghost of a smile flitted across the man's pallid face, but it was gone as quickly as it had appeared. 'Sorry, but—er—I don't happen to have a name,' he said quietly.

'Then you'd better find one,' Biggles told him shortly. 'We like to know our friends.'

'I must refer you to headquarters—somebody should be here to meet me. Ah! Here comes Major Raymond.'

Biggles pushed back his flying-helmet and received the major with a suspicious frown. 'What's going on, sir?' he asked.

'It's all right, Bigglesworth,' the major assured him quietly.

'I'm not so sure that it is, sir,' Biggles flung back belligerently. 'Who is this fellow?'

'He is one of our men.'

'One of *your* men? You mean he's a sp—agent?'

The major nodded.

'But—how did he know where to come to be picked up?'

'I told him.'

'*You* told him?'

'Yes.'

'But how . . . ?'

'Carrier pigeon*.'

Biggles flushed. Then his face paled. 'Then, if you'll permit me to express an opinion, sir, I don't think that's good enough,' he said angrily. 'Nothing was said about *this* in our plans. If we're caught now it will be a firing party for us**.'

'I'm sorry, Bigglesworth, but the exigencies of war made it imperative that we should get this man out of Germany immediately. And while not depreciating the good job of work you have done, may I remind you that he has taken bigger risks than you have—of facing

* Carrier pigeons were used by both sides for getting a message through enemy lines before the days of radio telephones.
** Anyone caught transporting or having transported a spy was treated as a spy himself and executed by firing squad.

a firing party? And to settle any grievance you may think you have, it may be some small comfort to you to know that, in bringing this fellow out, you four have done more good for our side to-day than any four men in the British army. I shall see that it is not overlooked. I'll talk to you later. That's all.' The major raised his hand in salute and, with his companion, walked quickly towards the squadron office.

Biggles took a cigarette from his case and tapped it on the back of his hand. 'The trouble with this perishing war is that you never know what you're doing,' he said bitterly. 'Come on, we might as well go and get some food.'

# Chapter 12
# Cutting It Fine

The business of the spy, or rather, the manner in which
the rescue flight had been used by Intelligence Headquarters while being kept in ignorance of the facts,
rankled with Biggles for the remainder of the day, and
he was only mollified when, that evening, Major Raymond came over to the squadron and gave his assur-
ance that it should not happen again. He did not say
that the rescue flight could not be used for Intelligence
purposes, but he promised that when this happened
the members of the flight should be informed.

In the quiet of his room Biggles talked to Thirty and
Rip. 'You see, you fellows are not even officers. Really,
you are civilians under arms, and if you were caught
you'd have your backs against a brick wall inside twelve
hours. I know, of course, that the Germans do not know
you are civilians; but supposing you were captured and
sent to a prison camp, and then some time later the
truth leaked out, in the English newspapers, for
instance, which are seen in Germany; well, they'd just
shoot you out of hand, and you couldn't blame them
for it. That's why I object to this being kept in the
dark as to Raymond's real scheme. And make no mistake; sooner or later the Boche is bound to get wind of
what is going on.'

Nothing more was said, in fact there was little to
say, so they continued their operations as planned.

They heard no more of the man they had brought out of Germany.

During the next few days they visited each of the picking-up points, and without particular incident rescued five British officers, one of whom was an infantry colonel of importance. After this they took three days' rest, but on their next trip everything seemed to go wrong from the beginning.

One of the officers whom they had rescued, a cavalry captain, had told them that he had reason to suppose that another officer would shortly succeed in getting out of the same prison camp; and if he did, in fact, succeed in getting out, he would be certain to make for the landing-ground—which happened to be aerodrome C—where he, the cavalry captain, had been picked up.

This was the first occasion on which the rescue flight had gone over with good reason to suppose that an escaped prisoner would be waiting to be picked up. Actually, they were not due at aerodrome C for another three days, but in the circumstances they decided to make a special flight, although, as parcels of food had by now been hidden in the northern hedge of each landing-ground, they did not think that the man would suffer any great hardships while he was waiting— beyond, of course, a good deal of anxiety.

A sequence of unforeseen, although quite natural, events made them late. As they were crossing the lines the Bristol's oil-pressure suddenly went wrong, and Thirty had no alternative but to return. Ten minutes sufficed to put it right, so Biggles, after a moment's hesitation, decided to carry on. On the next attempt a close burst of archie hurtled a piece of shrapnel into Algy's engine, and after signalling that he could not go on he turned and glided towards home. Thirty did not see him go, and was only aware of what had happened when Biggles came close and signalled to him to go on.

Twenty minutes later the two machines were attacked by three Pfalz Scouts*; the attack was only half-hearted, rather suggesting that the three enemy scout pilots were beginnners; still, a fight ensued, and this delayed the two rescue planes still further. As soon as they saw that they were outmatched, the three Germans broke off the fight by diving for the ground, where, in the circumstances, Biggles did not pursue them, although it looked as if they would provide him with two or three easy victories.

With one thing and another it was broad daylight by the time the two machines reached their objective, and both Biggles and Thirty, although unaware that they were thinking alike, were hoping that it would not be necessary to land. But, surely enough, a piece of paper blowing about in a corner of the field told them that their man was waiting.

Then, to his surprise and consternation, Thirty, as he landed, saw two men break cover, from different places, and stand waiting for him. He guessed at once what had happened. Two prisoners, each unaware of the other's presence, had arrived at the landing-ground. He had wondered vaguely once or twice what would happen in such an emergency, but no definite rule had been laid down, so it was with considerable misgiving that he taxied towards the point on which they were converging. He saw that both wore ragged British uniforms, one an ordinary infantry field-service tunic and

* Very successful German single-seater fighter with two or three machine guns synchronised to fire through the propeller.

the other an R.F.C. double-breasted tunic. He also noticed that the flying officer was limping. Standing up in the cockpit, he spoke to them together. 'I can't take you both,' he called.

An altercation immediately ensued, and from it these facts emerged. The infantry officer was a guards major; he wore the ribbon of the D.S.O.* on his tunic. The R.F.C. officer, a second-lieutenant, had not yet been taken prisoner. He was the pilot of an F.E. bomber which had been shot down on a raid only a few hours previously. His observer had been killed outright by the archie burst that caused their downfall; he, the pilot, had been wounded in the leg by the same burst. He knew nothing of the rescue flight. By the merest fluke he had been hiding in a ditch, in order to try to get back through the lines, but seeing two British machines he had, not unnaturally, exposed himself.

Thirty made up his mind quickly. 'I'm sorry, sir, but I shall have to take this chap first,' he told the major. 'He's wounded, and needs medical attention.'

'But I've been here for two days,' expostulated the guards officer, a heavily built, florid-faced man with an upturned moustache. Something in his manner annoyed Thirty.

'I can't help that, sir,' he said evenly. 'With a wounded officer in question I am surprised that you do not agree with me.'

'I have reasons for getting back,' snapped the major, making as if he would climb into the machine.

Major or no major, this was more than Thirty was

* Distinguished Service Order, a medal.

prepared to stand. 'I don't doubt that,' he replied curtly. 'So have we all. Stand away, please.'

The guards officer glared. 'You'll obey my orders,' he exclaimed wrathfully, and started climbing on to the wing.

Thirty whipped his Very pistol out of its pocket and levelled it. His face was pale, and there was a curious glitter in his eyes. 'If you don't get off that wing, I'll shoot you,' he snapped, in a voice that was as cold and brittle as ice. 'I'll show you who is in command here.'

The major stepped back. 'You'd threaten *me*?' he gasped incredulously. 'I'll have you put under close arrest the moment I get back.'

'It will be some time before you are in a position to do that if you go on talking in that strain,' Thirty told him. Then, to the R.F.C. officer, 'In you get. Give him a hand, Rip.'

The major burst into a stream of profanity, but Thirty cut him short. 'Stand clear, please,' he shouted. 'I can't stay here arguing.'

The major suddenly changed his tune. 'Will you come back for me?' he asked.

'Yes.'

'When?'

'To-morrow morning at dawn.'

'But they'll retake me before then,' declared the major desperately. 'The fellows in the camp won't be able to keep my disappearance a secret for more than a day or two at the most, and then they'll have the dogs on my track. I mustn't be retaken. You see—I—killed a sentry to get out.'

Thirty, hand on the throttle, stared. 'Great heavens!' he breathed. 'All right,' he said crisply. 'Get back in the ditch. I'll be back in two hours—unless I'm shot down on the way.'

Biggles was roaring low overhead. Thirty glanced up, realizing that he would be at a loss to understand the delay. He waited no longer. The Bristol's propeller took on an added sheen as he opened the throttle, and the waving grass flattened under the tearing slipstream. A minute later his wheels, still spinning, had left the ground, and he had taken up position beside Biggles, the two machines rising and falling lightly in the slight bumps caused by the freshening breeze.

They flew low all the way to the lines, hoping in this way to escape observation by the enemy scouts who, by this time, would certainly be on the move. They saw Mahoney's flight in the distance, no doubt looking for them higher up, but Mahoney did not see them. Knowing that he was well able to take care of himself Thirty did not worry much on that account, and shortly afterwards he was on the aerodrome, running to meet Biggles.

'What happened?' asked Biggles, tersely.

'Awful mess. There were two of them; a guards major and one of our chaps who has been hit in the leg. I brought him first.'

'Quite right.'

'The major was savage about it. He has threatened to put me under arrest when he gets back.'

'Then let him find his own way back,' replied Biggles promptly.

'I can't do that; I've promised to fetch him.'

'When?'

'Now.'

'*Now?*'

'Yes.'

'You're crazy.'

'I know—but he got a promise out of me. I think he's got the wind up because he killed a sentry getting out of jail.'

Biggles started. 'By gosh! That's bad,' he muttered. 'They'll hang him for that if they get him. Looks as if we shall have to try to fetch him.' He swung round on his heel. 'Hi! Smyth!' he shouted to the flight-sergeant. 'Fill up both machines and make it snappy.'

'You needn't come, Biggles,' began Thirty, but Biggles cut him short.

'Don't be a fool,' he snapped. 'You can't go over there alone. Here's Mahoney coming in, cursing like a trooper, I bet, because we gave him the slip. He'll come part of the way with us. We've just time for a coffee while they're filling up.'

They ran down to the mess, burnt their mouths with hot coffee, and then hurried back to the sheds, where they explained to the indignant Mahoney what had happened. 'You fill up and then come to meet us,' Biggles told him, as he clambered up into his tiny cockpit. 'Come on, Thirty, let's get it over. Keep your eyes open and your gun ready, Rip. Is your machine all right now, Algy?'

'Yes.'

'Are you coming with us?'

'I'm not likely to stay behind.'

'Fine. Let's get along, then.'

The sun was high in the sky as the three machines took off and headed straight for their objective. And for a time it looked as if they might reach it without being molested, for the only hostile aircraft they saw was a two-seater that made off when the pilot saw them coming.

They were within five miles of the landing-ground when Rip struck Thirty on the shoulder.

Thirty looked round. Rip pointed. Following the out-stretched hand Thirty saw a number of tiny specks far behind them. There were five or six, he was not sure which, so far away were they and so close together did they fly.

Rip leaned over, and cupping his hands round his mouth, yelled in Thirty's ear, 'They're following us.'

Thirty nodded to show that he understood. He saw Biggles and Algy both look round, and then at each other. Biggles's Camel surged forward until it was just in front of, and not more than ten feet away from, the Bristol's port wing-tip, with Biggles making unmistakable signs to Thirty that he was to go on.

Without another glance behind, Thirty put his nose down and dived for the landing-field, which he could now see in the distance. He knew that everything now was a matter of time. If he could get down and pick up his passenger before they were overtaken there was a chance that he might fight his way home, but if the enemy scouts caught him first it would be hopeless to attempt to land.

Reaching the field he turned into the wind and then side-slipped down steeply, and in spite of the desperate situation a faint smile crept over his face as he saw the guards officer standing out in the field as if he owned it. Wondering subconsciously whether the officer was a brave man or a fool, Thirty flattened out and landed. Possibly it was due to his haste, but, for the first time, he made a bad landing. Or he may have touched a rut, or a molehill. He never knew. But he held his breath as the Bristol bounced like a rubber ball, and he waited for the shock of it to come down again, fully expecting the undercarriage to crumple. Normally, in such circumstances he would have opened up his engine and gone round again, but now there was no time for such a proceeding.

Bump... bump... bump. The undercarriage creaked as the Bristol finally settled on the ground in a manner that would have disgraced a pupil at a flying training school, but it stood the strain, and Thirty, gasping his relief, pushed up his goggles.

There was no need for him to taxi up to his passenger, for the major was less than a hundred yards away and sprinting towards him, so he seized the opportunity of looking at what was happening in the air.

Less than a mile away were five enemy scouts, noses down and tails high.

The two Camels had turned to meet them, and even as Thirty watched, the enemy formation split up for individual action. From the way they flew he knew that the pilots were old hands, and his heart went cold with anxiety. However, he could do nothing about it; he could not even watch what happened. With the roar of racing engines and the chatter of machine-guns in his ears, he watched Rip help the major into the cockpit. Such was his haste that he fell in head first.

Thirty waited no longer. His man was aboard, and the Bristol swung round for a down-wind take-off. There was no time to taxi to the far side of the field to get into the wind.

Tail up, he was speeding down the wind when an Albatros struck the ground in a sheet of flame immediately in front of him. Instinctively he kicked the rudder-bar, and as quickly gave himself up for lost as the Bristol's wing touched the grass in the frightful swerve that resulted. Fortunately the herbage was sparse or the plane must have gone over. As it was, the machine righted itself and raced on towards the hedge. But it was still on the ground.

Thirty was well aware of the danger of a down-wind take-off at any time, but now, with a numbing horror inside him, he remembered that the Bristol had three passengers instead of the two for which it was designed. The hedge seemed to float towards him. His hand tightened on the joystick and the Bristol reluctantly unstuck, only to touch the ground again a few yards farther on. Had the wheels encountered the slightest obstruction at that moment the Bristol would have turned several somersaults before spreading the fragments of itself all over the field. Fortunately for its occupants the ground was clear.

Thirty saw the hedge immediately in front of him. He did the only thing left to do. With his lips pressed together in a straight line, slowly but firmly he pulled the joystick back. Lurching like a drunken man, the Bristol rose. There was a whip-like *swish* as its wheels ripped through the thin twigs on the top of the hedge, nearly pulling the machine into the ground on the other side. Then the whirling propeller lifted the nose and the machine rose slowly into the air.

Thirty dared not look behind. He dared not look anywhere but straight in front of him, for his nerves were at breaking-point from shock and the machine demanded all his attention. Twice he flinched as Rip's gun spoke, and once he caught a momentary glimpse of a red-nosed scout in his reflector.

Not until he was at a thousand feet and on a course for home did he risk a brief inspection of the atmosphere. But he could see little—only a small group of zooming and banking machines far behind him. Thirty did not attempt to climb higher. Speed, he knew, was the only chance, so he put his nose down and began the method of travel known to pilots as hedge-hopping, regarding dispassionately the stampeding cattle, or even human beings, over which he passed.

A quarter of an hour later he became aware of four Camels just above him, and he recognized Mahoney's flight. He did not see where they came from. Nor did he care particularly. He was only conscious of a feeling of great satisfaction.

Just before they reached the lines he discovered that the Camels had disappeared as mysteriously as they had arrived. Not until an hour later did he learn that they had turned off to meet an enemy formation that was diving on to the lone Bristol.

Approaching the lines, he had an unpleasant five minutes as an archie on the ground opened up on him. For the first time he actually saw the faces of the gunners as they stared up at him. A balloon cable gave him a severe fright, for he had forgotten that there were such things and he nearly flew into it. Of the hundreds of shots that he knew were fired at him as he roared low across the trenches, only one hit his machine; he saw the hole a minute or two later, through his wing, near the fuselage.

On no previous flight had Thirty felt so completely exhausted as he did when the Bristol finally ran to a halt near to where the mechanics were waiting for him. They ran by the wing-tips until he was on the tarmac, when he switched off and dropped wearily to the ground.

Pushing up his goggles, he turned a pair of red-rimmed eyes to the major, who had followed Rip to the ground. 'I hope you enjoyed your flip,' he said coldly, and turned his face to the east so that he could watch for the others to return.

A few minutes later he heard the drone of the Camel's Bentley engines. Five came in in a ragged formation. Biggles, Algy, and Mahoney were among them. Mahoney had lost a man.

Biggles came across to where Thirty was waiting. 'Where's your passenger?' he asked.

Thirty looked round in surprise. 'Well, I'm dashed!' he said. 'He's gone.'

'Nice polite sort of cove,' grinned Algy. 'Oh, forget him. Let's go and get a bit of lunch. I reckon we've earned it.'

# Chapter 13
# Disaster

At eight o'clock the following morning Major Raymond arrived at the aerodrome. Biggles saw his Crossley tender coming up the track that led to the officers' mess, where the members of the rescue flight who were not doing a show that morning were making a leisurely breakfast.

'Here comes Raymond,' Biggles told the others. 'Feeling in a prophetic mood, I'm prepared to wager that he is coming to see us.'

Biggles was correct. Two minutes later Major Raymond came into the dining-room. ''Morning,' he said briefly. 'I saw the C.O. outside; he told me you were in here. Mind if I join you in a cup of coffee? I was on the move early.'

Biggles pulled out a chair as Algy operated the coffee-pot.

For a moment or two nobody spoke. The major stirred his coffee thoughtfully.

'Well?' murmured Biggles.

'Well—what?' returned the major.

Biggles smiled. 'Am I right in assuming that you haven't come all the way from Wing Headquarters just to wish us good morning?'

'You are,' answered the major.

'Bad news?'

'In a way, yes; but nothing to do with you.'

Thirty breathed again. For one horrible moment he had thought that something had happened to Forty.

'I've got a very sticky job for somebody,' continued the major. 'In fact, it's so sticky that I hardly like to *ask* anybody to do it, much less order him—not that there is any question of ordering. It's essentially a job for a volunteer.'

'Bad as that, eh?'

'Worse—if anything.'

'If we knew what it was we could tell you if it was in our line,' murmured Biggles.

'Quite. That's why I've come here. The dickens of it is, I've got no right to tell you what I shall *have* to tell you. You know without my telling you that the one thing that really matters in espionage is secrecy. If one of my agents happened to walk in here at this minute he wouldn't recognize me.'

'*Must* you tell us—this secret?'

'It wouldn't be fair to ask you to do the job without telling you the precise facts.'

Biggles shrugged his shoulders slightly. 'You know best, sir.'

The major leaned forward, his voice dropping to a whisper. 'If any one here even mentions one word of what I am going to say he might be responsible for the death of thousands of our troops.'

Biggles looked grave. 'I'd rather not know anything about it,' he muttered in a worried tone.

The major made a gesture of helplessness. 'I *must* tell you,' he said again, as if he hated the idea. 'Listen. You know the village of Belville-sur-Somme? It's on the other side of the lines now; the Huns took it from us in their big push last autumn.'

'I know it,' Biggles nodded. 'Our artillery has knocked the village about, but by a curious fluke the church tower hasn't been touched.'

'That is not a fluke.'

'No?'

'No. Knowing that we should lose the village, some alterations were made in that church tower last year. It's a *square* tower, you remember. One wall of it is hollow. We've a man stationed in it.'

Biggles's eyes opened wide, but he said nothing.

'Yes,' continued the major; 'he sits up there all day, in the centre of the enemy's position—telling us everything. Or rather, he did tell us until yesterday.'

'Ah! They've got him?'

'No. We laid an underground telegraph. The transmitter at his end has gone wrong; a part has burnt out. He needs a spare.'

'And somebody has got to take it to him?' put in Biggles evenly.

'Precisely.'

'Have you lost touch with him?'

'Of course. We lost touch the moment his instrument broke down.'

'Then how did you know it had broken down?'

'He had a pigeon—just one, for emergency.'

'Pity; he should have had more.'

'No. They would have cooed, and perhaps given him away. A cooing pigeon has been the death signal for more than one agent.'

'The job's urgent?'

'Every hour's delay is costing us men. Having had the man there, we are blind without him.'

'This sounds like a one-man job,' observed Biggles gravely.

'Yes.'

'How will the one who goes be able to identify the chap at the other end?'

'Easily. He's the village padre—a priest—Father Dupont. The difficulty will be to get to him without being questioned. If *you* went and were questioned— well, it would be all over, since I believe I am right in saying that you do not speak German fluently?'

'*I* do,' declared Thirty. 'I've lived in Germany.'

'By Jove! I didn't know that,' said the major tersely.

'I'll go,' offered Thirty. 'I stand the best chance of anybody of getting through.'

Biggles looked at him with serious, thoughtful eyes. 'No one can deny that,' he said slowly. 'You know what will happen if you're—'

'If I'm caught? Of course. It can't be helped. Some one will have to take the risk.'

'That's the only way of looking at it,' murmured the major.

He put his hand in his pocket and took out a small oblong package. 'Here's the thing,' he said, passing it to Thirty. 'There is no need for me to say any more. We shall soon know if our man gets it. Whatever happens, don't give *him* away. I'll leave the rest to you. Good luck.' The major rose and held out his hand to Thirty. Then, without another word, he went.

'It looks to me as if we started more than we bargained for when we started this rescue business,' observed Biggles, sadly. 'How are you proposing to handle this, Thirty?'

'I think the safest plan would be to go over at night;

132

there would be less chance of being seen in the dark. I'll land at aerodrome C, which I reckon is only a few miles behind Belville, taking an old macintosh with me to cover up my uniform. If Rip comes with me he can fly the machine home as soon as he has put me on the ground—unless he cares to wait. Maybe it would be better to go, and come back the next morning early; or if I'm not back, the next day.'

'I'll wait,' declared Rip firmly.

Biggles shook his head. 'I don't like it,' he muttered.

'I can't say that I'm enthusiastic about it myself, but we couldn't very well refuse to go,' admitted Thirty.

'When are you going?' asked Algy.

'Might as well go to-night,' answered Thirty. 'You heard what Major Raymond said about urgency.'

'And you'll wait for him, Rip?' questioned Biggles.

'Yes.'

'It's a fair step from aerodrome C to Belville,' Biggles pointed out. 'I think you'd better compromise. Give him, say, four hours. If he isn't back by then, come home, and then we'll all go over every morning until we do get him. All sorts of contingencies might arise. He may be delayed. Somebody might come along while you are waiting. But there is this about it—we all know where he is and what he is doing; provided he doesn't run into trouble, it would only be a question of time before we picked him up. It's difficult to work to a fixed time. What do you think, Thirty?'

'I agree. Let Rip wait for a time by all means, so long as everything is quiet. But it might suit me better if I knew that if I was hung up he'd go home.'

'Then there seems to be nothing else to discuss,' said Biggles, getting up from the table. 'Let's go and have a look over the Bristol. You might take a packet of food to hide in the hedge. By the way, if any one else turns up—prisoners, I mean—they'll have to wait until this show is finished. We can't do half a dozen things at once.'

After that they went up to the sheds and spent the remainder of the day doing such jobs as were likely to be useful, occasionally discussing minor details of the mission. Twilight fell while they were at dinner, and as soon as the meal was over Thirty and Rip collected their kit and, accompanied by Biggles and Algy, who came to see them off, made their way slowly to the sheds. All the pilots of 266 squadron were home, and their machines put away for the night. Only the dark-painted Bristol stood on the tarmac. They hung about until it got properly dark, when Thirty made preparations for departure.

'I ought to be doing this job, you know,' Biggles told him, with a worried frown.

'You'd probably do the flying part better than I shall, but what you'd gain by that you'd lose by not being able to speak German sufficiently well to pass for a native,' returned Thirty. 'You ready, Rip?'

The small parcel of food was put into the rear cockpit, and Thirty and Rip climbed into their seats.

'You know the colour of the night?' asked Biggles.

'Yes.'

'Cheerio, then. Remember, if anything goes wrong, don't leave aerodrome C. That's where we will look for you.'

Rip nodded, waved his hand, and switched on, for Algy was waiting by the propeller. The engine started. Algy pulled the chocks away and the machine moved forward into the darkness. A moment later it was in the air, heading for its objective.

Thirty climbed fairly high before crossing the lines, for he was particularly anxious to avoid the search-lights. It seemed to him that there were more than usual, and they flashed in a peculiar way. Then he saw the reason. Lightning was flashing across the sky in several places, and he experienced a pang of uneasiness; a thunderstorm was something he had not taken into his calculations, but it did not occur to him to turn back. Which is not to say that he would not have done so had he known that less than twenty miles away huts were being uprooted and hangars blown flat by the violence of the tempest. He eased the stick forward a little and raced on, aware that his compass was behaving oddly, although he was not altogether surprised, for he was well aware of the influence a magnetic storm can have on delicate instruments.

Thirty reckoned that he was still about ten miles from aerodrome C when the first spot of rain lashed his face. The sky had turned black, with no sign of a star; there were no more searchlights, but at frequent intervals the heavens were lacerated by vivid flashes of lightning, which showed up the earth clearly, enabling him more than once to identify a landmark. He was worried, but still it did not occur to him to return with his mission unfulfilled. A prolonged flash showed him the landing-field, so he throttled back and glided down towards it, more than a little thankful that the storm had not yet broken; indeed, he had begun to hope that it would pass over.

He was now very low, straining his eyes down into the gloom below, holding the machine off as long as he dared, hoping for another flash of lightning to show him the way in. Instead, the storm broke. In an instant he was fighting his way through blinding rain.

He ought to have turned back. He knew that he was taking a terrible risk, but an obstinate streak in him made him persist in his landing. He could just see the ground and the black shadows which he knew were trees. Passing between two trees, he flattened out, confident that he was down safely. Just as the wheels touched, the lightning flashed and the world was flooded with a brilliant blue light.

It showed Thirty everything about him, but he was only concerned with two of the objects he saw. Ten yards in front of the bumping machine stood a man with his arms outstretched. A little farther on loomed a thick-set hedge.

For the next second, which to Thirty seemed like eternity, he did not think. His brain seemed to have become paralysed. It made no difference. It was too late to do anything. His only real thought, and this was subconscious, was that he had come down in the wrong field. There was a violent crash as the lurching machine struck the figure. Instinctively, knowing that he was going to crash, Thirty flicked off the ignition to prevent fire. There was a rending, grinding crash as the Bristol bored into the hedge. Then, suddenly, silence— silence broken only by the teeming rain and the intermittent roll of thunder.

For a split second Thirty sat still, stunned by the calamity. Then, recovering himself with a rush, he undid his safety belt, flung it off, and turned to Rip.

'Well, here we are,' said Rip, coolly.

'I know it,' snapped Thirty. 'I wish we weren't.

What are we going to do? Heavens! Did you ever see such rain in your life?'

'What about that poor devil you knocked over?' shouted Rip, above the tearing wind which now struck the wrecked machine like a tornado.

Thirty did not answer. He jumped down and fought his way through the storm to where the figure lay motionless.

Rip joined him. 'You've killed him,' he yelled.

Thirty knelt, his hands groping. Then he sprang to his feet, laughing hysterically. 'It's a scarecrow,' he cried. 'We're in the wrong field.'

The wind became a thousand shrieking demons clutching at them, slashing the rain into their faces, making it difficult for them to keep their feet.

'We would choose a night like this,' yelled Thirty bitterly in Rip's ear.

'What are you going to do? We can't stand out here like a pair of fools in this rain,' cried Rip, wildly.

Thirty, crouching low, made his way back to the machine. He grabbed Rip's arm. 'Get that grub out,' he shouted.

'Why?'

'I'm going to set fire to her. She'll be seen a mile off when it gets light. If I burn her there'll be nothing left to see. Now's the time. Every one will be indoors, and the fire won't be seen for a hundred yards, anyway, in this perishing rain.'

Rip climbed into the wreck and dragged out the parcel of food. Thirty managed to find his Very pistol in the torn cockpit. 'Stand back,' he yelled, and sent the flaming charge into the Bristol's main tank. Then he hurled the pistol into the leaping flames that gushed out, and ran down the hedge to get clear of the bullets that he knew would start flying in all directions as soon as the flames reached the ammunition.

Satisfied that they were in a safe place, he stopped. 'There is only one thing to do,' he told Rip.

'What's that?'

'You get across to the proper landing-field. It's just over there, to the right. Wait for Biggles. He'll guess that the storm has jiggered us. If he comes before I'm back tell him what happened.'

'Before you're back . . . what are you going to do?'

'I'm going on to find the padre.'

'What—in your uniform? You're mad. Great Scott! Where's the macintosh you were going to wear? Did you bring one?'

Thirty staggered. His hand went to his brow. 'My God! I left it in the machine,' he choked. 'Quick!' He spun round.

But it was too late. Already the ill-fated Bristol was enveloped in flames from end to end. Helpless, they stood on the outskirts of the ruddy glow of the flames and watched it burn. Cartridges began exploding and forced them to take cover again.

'I must be crazy,' groaned Thirty. 'What on earth could I have been thinking about to do a fool thing like that?'

'You were upset by the crash, I expect.'

'Yes, I must have been. But what am I going to do? I can't walk about the roads like this and hope to get away with it. By gosh! I've got it. The scarecrow!'

Risking the bullets, Thirty tore across to where the dummy figure lay. 'A peasant's old blue blouse—the very thing!' he cried exultantly, and started dragging

138

the scarecrow towards the hedge. Reaching it, he dragged off his flying-kit and then donned the one whole garment that comprised the scarecrow's attire, a loose blue calico blouse of the sort that is commonly worn by the working classes in France and Belgium. It was, of course, saturated, but he was already so wet that it made little difference.

'Got the box of tricks you've got to hand over to the padre?' questioned Rip, anxiously.

'Yes—in my pocket. I'm off now. I've wasted too much time here already. You find your way to the northern hedge of the landing-field and wait.'

'I'd rather come with you.'

'We haven't two blouses, so it's no use talking about that,' answered Thirty, shortly. 'I hope I'll be back about dawn.'

Rip held out his hand. He seemed to be choking. 'Goodbye, Thirty,' he said huskily. 'Be careful.'

'I will,' Thirty assured him. 'Remember the motto.'

'What . . . ?'

'Thick and thin.'

'Thick and thin,' echoed Rip hoarsely.

Thirty waved his hand and set off down the hedge at a steady trot.

Rip watched him until he disappeared into the darkness, and then, picking up the food-bag, began to make his way cautiously towards the landing-field.

# Chapter 14
# Belville-Sur-Somme

Thirty struck off across the fields until he came to the road he was looking for; he knew of its existence, having previously marked it down from the air; he also knew that in one direction it led to Belville-sur-Somme, some six or seven kilometres distant.

At the road he halted for a minute or two to take stock of the general situation. The centre of the storm had now passed and with it the torrential downpour, although lightning still flickered along the eastern horizon and the aftermath of the rainclouds precipitated a steady drizzle. The night was dark. From where he stood, soaked to the skin, he could not see a single light. Fortunately it was not cold, so he suffered no great discomfort on account of the wet. Satisfied with his inspection of the immediate surroundings, he set off at a steady pace towards the village.

He had covered about a kilometre when he heard a motor vehicle coming along the road behind him; it sounded like a heavy lorry. It was, in fact, a motor-wagon, and he stood aside to allow it to pass, for the road was so narrow that it occupied the whole of it, and the wheels were spurting mud on either side. He did not attempt to hide; there seemed to be no reason why he should; the driver of the vehicle would expect to see somebody on the road occasionally, and there was no reason why he should attach any importance to a belated peasant. Therefore Thirty simply stood aside to allow the wagon to pass.

It did not occur to him that it might stop, so he was unprepared for what happened. As it drew level with him the wagon slowed down, and too late Thirty wished that he had hidden in the hedge until it had passed; but he realized that to do so now would be foolish, for the headlights had revealed him.

'Lovely night,' called the driver, with cheerful sarcasm, speaking in German. 'How far are you going?'

Thirty, in the brief interval at his disposal before he was compelled to answer, could think of no reason for not telling the truth. 'Belville,' he said.

'So am I,' declared the driver. 'Hop up.'

Thirty hopped up. There was nothing else he could do. As the wagon lurched forward he snatched a glance at his companion, and saw that he was a soldier.

'Nearly time this cursed war was over,' grumbled the driver.

Thirty agreed, without enthusiasm. He was thinking hard.

The driver looked at him for a moment; it could only be for a moment because care was needed to keep the vehicle on the narrow road. 'What are you doing, wandering about by yourself on a night like this?' he questioned, but without real interest.

'I've got a message to deliver,' replied Thirty, evasively.

Silence fell.

'It's a fair step to Belville; lucky for you I came along,' observed the German presently, in an inconsequential tone of voice, apparently for the sake of saying something.

'Yes, it will save my legs and my boot-leather,' agreed Thirty, wishing the man would not talk.

'Got a match on you?' was the next question.

Thirty had, but he did not say so, for the very good reason that he had no desire to reveal what was under his blouse. 'I don't smoke,' he answered truthfully, and the German accepted this as a negative answer.

Presently, to Thirty's relief, the soldier began to sing. The wagon trundled on, sometimes passing a farmhouse or peasant's cottage. Once they passed what looked like a big concentration camp. Shortly afterwards lights began to appear ahead.

The driver stopped singing and yawned. 'Nearly there,' he said. 'Where shall I drop you?'

It struck Thirty that he was safer where he was than he would be on the ground, for they were now meeting frequent parties of soldiers, no doubt on their way back to the concentration camp after an evening in the village. 'Do you go near the church?' he asked.

'I'm parking in the square right in front of it,' announced the German.

'Then there's no need for you to stop; I'll go there with you,' returned Thirty, well satisfied with this arrangement.

They entered the long village street, ran the full length of it, bumped across a level crossing, and then turned into a large square on the far side of which loomed the black silhouette of the church tower.

Thirty caught his breath and held it, for the scene was very different from the one he had imagined. He had thought to dismount in a deserted village square whence he would be able to stroll away without further parley. Instead of that he found himself in the centre

142

of a scene of military activity. Parked all round the square were lorries and several sorts of artillery. Horses were picketed with cavalry precision; round them, stable-guards in oilskins or great-coats kept the animals in order. In one corner the fire of a field-kitchen flung a cheerful glow over the shining cobble-stones. Troops crowded round it. Soldiers were everywhere.

Into the very middle of this unwelcome spectacle the driver guided his wagon. It stopped with a jerk. '*So*,' he said. 'Here we are.'

'Thanks, I'll do as much for you some day,' said Thirty quietly, and prepared to dismount. In spite of his efforts to remain calm, his heart was fluttering, and he determined to lose no time in removing himself from such distasteful surroundings.

But even as he climbed down a cloaked figure detached itself from a group and moved towards the vehicle.

'Is that you, Willy Schmidt?' asked a voice.

'*Ja*,' replied the driver.

'Who's that you've got with you?'

'A fellow I gave a lift to, that's all.'

'You know it's against orders to give rides to strangers.'

'He's the son of the woman at my billet,' lied the soldier, evidently with the object of saving himself from further reprimand.

Thirty began to walk away. Every instinct in him was prompting him to run, but he kept himself under control and walked as naturally as possible. Risking a sidelong glance, he saw to his consternation that the German N.C.O. was staring at his feet; he knew well enough what the man was staring at, and only by a supreme effort did he refrain from looking down at his field-boots.

'Hi, you!' shouted the N.C.O. suddenly.

Thirty pretended not to hear. Mingling with a party of soldiers, he hurried amongst them, and then slipped between the line of lorries to the pavement.

The N.C.O. shouted again, louder this time. Thirty heard him start to run forward and knew that he was in a tight corner. To make a bolt for it would, he knew, attract attention to himself, and with so many troops about this was the last thing he wanted. Still walking as quickly as he dared, his eyes flashed round his immediate surroundings. A dozen paces away a narrow alley leading off the square beckoned invitingly, and towards it he turned his steps. As soon as he was inside he darted forward, and did not slow down until the darkness in the unlighted passage forced him to go more warily.

He stopped to listen. He could still hear the N.C.O.'s strident voice, but he judged that he was talking to the troops in the square and had not followed him into the alley. Not a little relieved, he looked about him; he knew that he must be close to the church, but owing to the narrowness of the path in which he found himself, all he could see was the rising walls of the dingy houses on either side. However, to go back was out of the question, so he hurried on, keeping a look-out for an opening on either hand, hoping that he would find one wide enough to enable him to see the church tower and thus get his bearings. Instead, he came upon something which suited him even better, although it was not without a grim significance, for at the point where he struck it there was a surprising number of newly turned mounds of earth. It was the churchyard. In the centre of it loomed the stately mass of the church itself, now gaunt and forbidding in the dim light. Beyond it, and a little to one side, stood a house, from one window of which, on the ground-floor, a blur of orange light glowed fitfully through the misty rain.

Standing as it did in the churchyard, he knew that the house could be nothing but the presbytery, but between him and the little path that led to it was a formidable fence of perpendicular iron railings. He hesitated, and while he stood thus in indecision he heard footsteps approaching from the direction from which he had come. The footsteps were hurried, and accompanied by the sound of many voices. Instinctively he started off the opposite way, but before he had gone a dozen paces he heard footsteps coming from that direction also. In a moment he was clambering over the railings, hampered not a little by the blue blouse which he dared not discard. Reaching the top, he balanced himself precariously for a moment, and then jumped down on the other side. He landed with a jar that shook most of the breath out of his body, for the ground was uneven; but, waiting only long enough to recover his balance, he sped across the churchyard like a hunted animal, jumping over graves and dodging round the ornate tombstones that rose in front of him.

He reached a shrubbery, which he now discovered formed a hedge between the churchyard and the presbytery garden, and there stopped to collect his wits and his composure, for his nerves were quivering under the strain of his predicament. He could still hear voices in the direction of the footpath, but otherwise all seemed quiet, so, moving quietly, he forced a way through the shrubbery and approached the house.

Now that the moment had come, doubts began to assail him. Suppose it was not the right house? Suppose the priest was not at home? Suppose . . . He pulled himself together with an effort. Should he go to the window, or to the door? Peering into the gloom, he saw that he was in a small paved courtyard, on the far side of which stood a door with a window on either side. No lights showed. All was as silent as the grave.

'Well, it's no use standing here; I've got to get in somehow,' he thought desperately, and walking quickly to the door, knocked on it with his knuckles. Then he listened; but the only sound was the monotonous drip-drip-drip of rain from the overflowing eaves. He knocked again, looking apprehensively over his shoulder in the direction of the path, where sounds suggested that a number of men had halted.

'Yes, what is it?'

Thirty jumped convulsively as the words, spoken softly in French, came from the doorway. He had not heard the door open. Even now he was not quite sure whether it was open or shut.

'Father Dupont?' he whispered.

'Yes, my son,' replied the voice evenly. 'What can I do for you at this late hour?'

'I have a message for you,' said Thirty softly, in his best French.

'Ah! Come in.'

Thirty stepped forward and stood still while he heard the door being closed and bolted. Suddenly a match flared up, and for the first time he could see the speaker, who was now lighting a candle. He experienced a feeling of profound relief when he perceived the black cassock of a priest.

'Follow me.'

Obediently Thirty followed the man down a narrow panelled corridor, on either side of which hung rows of old prints—pictures of saints and other religious subjects. Then a door was opened, and he found himself in a well-lighted room that was evidently a study.

'Kindly be seated.'

Thirty sat nervously in the proffered chair while the priest walked slowly to the chair behind his desk and settled himself in it. Thirty looked at him curiously, for he was not in any way the sort of man he expected to see. Vaguely, at the back of his mind, he had visualized a keen, hawk-like face with piercing eyes; a slim, sinister-looking person. Instead, he found himself looking into a pair of gentle brown eyes, as soft as those of a doe. They were set in a round, kindly face, free from any sign of care or worry. But for the clerical attire, the man might have been a prosperous restaurant-proprietor—so thought Thirty as he gazed at him, wondering how to open the conversation.

'You said something about a message, I think?' the priest reminded him, quietly.

Thirty groped for his pocket under the blouse, and took out the little box which he had risked so much to deliver. 'I was told to bring this to you,' he said, simply.

The priest's eyes looked at him from a face that was now completely devoid of expression. 'Thank you,' he said. 'Is that all?'

'Yes . . . that's all,' replied Thirty awkwardly, somewhat taken aback by the other's manner.

'Then you'll be going now? Come, I will show you out.'

Thirty stared. In his heart he knew that his mission had been accomplished and there was no reason for him to delay, yet he had hardly expected such a casual reception. Doubts again swept through him.

'You *are* Father Dupont?' he questioned, feeling more than a little embarrassed.

'Do you doubt it?'

'Er—no.'

'Then why question it?'

Thirty plunged. 'You know what is in that box?'

The priest regarded him dispassionately. 'I shall find out,' he said.

Thirty experienced a strange sensation of anti-climax. The encounter, so far from having any dramatic quality, had proved to be so casual as to make him feel suddenly foolish. A faint smile crossed his face. But it faded suddenly as a sound reached his ears, and he knew from the manner in which the priest stiffened almost imperceptibly that he had heard it, too. Otherwise his manner did not change. Footsteps were approaching the house—heavy footsteps; and with them, faintly, came the chink of spurs.

The priest looked at Thirty. 'Did any one see you come here?' he asked, in a low voice.

'No—that is, I don't think so.'

'Then go through into the kitchen. It is the first turning on the right down the corridor. Put on the apron you will find hanging behind the door and stir the soup which you will find simmering on the fire. Say nothing. Should any one speak to you, act as though you were dumb.' The priest spoke quietly, but swiftly.

148

Thirty nodded, and turning on his heel strode swiftly down the corridor. As he passed into the kitchen there came a loud knocking on the door.

# Chapter 15
# A Desperate Predicament

Acting almost mechanically, he unhooked the apron which he found hanging on the back of the door and slipped it on, also a white chef's hat which was with it. He had purposely left the door ajar, and with what tense interest he listened can be better imagined than described. A glance showed him the soup simmering on an old-fashioned stove, but he paid no further attention to it.

Standing just inside the kitchen with his ear to the slightly open door, he heard the front door opened; a word of greeting, spoken in German, followed.

'Ah, good evening, *Herr Leutnant\**,' said the priest, easily. 'What indiscretion have you enjoyed that you seek absolution at this—'

'I seek something more concrete than absolution,' broke in a voice, bluntly. 'A suspicious stranger was seen in the village not long ago. My corporal swears he made off in the direction of the churchyard, so I have looked in to warn you to keep your doors locked.'

'Surely this—er—stranger would not be so evil as to rob a poor priest like myself. My thanks for your solicitude, nevertheless.'

'One never knows,' returned the voice.

Thirty breathed more easily. It seemed as if the visit

* German rank equivalent to 2nd lieutenant.

portended nothing very serious, after all. But at the *Leutnant*'s next words he stiffened with horror. 'We've sent for the dogs; they'll soon rout him out,' muttered the German, viciously.

The dogs! The words so upset Thirty that he could not think clearly. He knew well enough what the *Leutnant* meant, for he had heard often enough of the sagacious police-dogs that were used by the German army. What upset him most was the knowledge that once the dogs were put on his trail they would follow him to the house, which, apart from his own undoing, could hardly fail to throw suspicion on the priest.

Thirty forced himself to think calmly. At all costs he must save the man upon whom so much depended. But how? He could think of only one way. Whether he was there or not, the dogs would certainly lead the Germans into the house. That was inevitable. But if he adopted the role of a thief it would give the priest an opportunity of denying any knowledge of him, which he would be unable to do if he, Thirty, continued to pose as a chef. His mind was soon made up. A thief he would be. Then, once clear of the house, it would matter little to the priest if he were caught or not.

The German and the priest were still talking in the study, but their tones were muffled and he could not hear the actual words. Without expecting to see any one, he peeped along the corridor, but stepped back again swiftly with palpitating heart when his eyes fell on two German soldiers standing just inside the front door, which had been left open. Fortunately, they were watching the churchyard, so their backs were towards him.

Thirty steadied himself and looked round. The difficulty was to find something to steal. The only thing one was likely to find in a kitchen was food; still, that would do, he reflected. It would look as if he, a fugitive, had broken in on account of hunger.

In the larder he found, amongst other things, bread, half a ham, cheese, and a small sack half full of potatoes. It was the work of a moment to turn the potatoes out on to the floor; and in their place he thrust all the foodstuffs he could lay hands on. Thus laden, he stepped back into the kitchen. Instantly there was a sharp tap on the window. With a start that he could not repress, he looked in the direction of the sound. A face surmounted by a spiked helmet was grinning at him through the glass.

Thirty turned cold, but he did not lose control of himself. As much from sheer desperation as any thought of playing a bold hand, he crossed to the window and opened it.

'What do you want?' he said, in tones which he strove to keep casual.

'Any soup in the pot?' asked the German.

'Of course,' replied Thirty. 'Have some?'

'You bet—and so will Hans.' A second German appeared at the window.

'Stay where you are,' Thirty told them. 'If you come in here I may get into trouble.' With hands that trembled in spite of himself, he unhooked two soup-basins from the dresser, filled them, and handed them to the waiting Germans. 'Don't be long over it,' he said, meaningly.

As he turned back into the room, wondering if it might not be better to stay after all, he heard a hound bay not far away. That decided him. What the Germans would think when he went out he did not know; perhaps they would be too occupied with the soup to think anything; he hoped so, fervently. As he picked up the bag of food he noticed in a corner a bucket full of kitchen garbage—potato-peelings, cabbage-stalks, and broken egg-shells. It gave him an idea, so, hitching the bag over his left shoulder and holding it in his left hand, with the other he picked up the pail. Thus laden he walked quickly to the back door.

'What have you got there?' asked one of the Germans.

'Rubbish,' answered Thirty promptly. 'Time I got rid of it.'

'Here, let me take it,' exclaimed the other, putting his soup-basin on the window-sill. 'There's no need for you to come out.'

Thirty inwardly cursed the German for his friendliness. 'I'd better take it,' he said. 'It has to go in a special pig-trough, and you'll never find it in the dark. You finish your soup by the time I come back.' With that he strode off down a footpath that led away to the left.

He had not the remotest idea of where the path ended; his one concern was to get clear of the house. Twice he collided with fruit-trees, and then found himself in what was undoubtedly a kitchen garden. A few more paces and his feet sank into soft earth, which told him he was off the path, and he was about to retrace his steps when a pandemonium of barks and howls broke out in the direction of the churchyard. It nearly sent him into a panic, for he realized instantly what it meant. The hounds had found his scent.

The knowledge sent him forward at a run, fully

prepared for a sentry's challenge. Nothing of the sort happened, however. Still clinging to his burden, he came to the end of the garden, and a hedge. There was no gate, and nothing to indicate what lay beyond the hedge. To get through it, burdened as he was, was obviously an impossibility, so he got rid of both the sack and the bucket by the simple expedient of dropping them in a cabbage patch, after which he attacked the hedge.

With his clothes torn and his face bleeding from more than one scratch, he arrived on the other side, where he discovered to his dismay that he had left a good part of his blue blouse amongst the thorns. Peering into the darkness, he tried to see what was in front of him. It appeared to be a wide black shadow, and he took a pace towards it, only to throw himself back as he learned the truth. It was a river. 'Of course it's a river,' he thought bitterly, remembering the name of the village. 'It must be the Somme.'

A fresh chorus of baying not far away settled any doubt in his mind as to which way to take. Consoling himself with the thought that the water would at least end his trail as far as the hounds were concerned, he lowered himself into the river and struck out for the opposite bank, which he could discern faintly some thirty yards away. But before he could reach it an entirely unlooked-for development occurred.

Out of the darkness on the far side of the river appeared a horse. He saw it without any particular surprise or alarm, and watched it as it walked slowly down the bank. Then something in its actions touched a chord in his memory. What on earth was the creature doing? Its movements suggested that it was pulling a heavy weight, but he could see nothing behind it. The horse passed on, still pulling its invisible burden.

He was still pondering on this phenomenon, without quickening his stroke, when something fell on his head. It also fell on the water beside him, but he was unaware of that, for the next instant the object that had fallen seemed to spring up under his jaw with a force that nearly dislocated it. And forthwith something tightened round his throat and began to drag him through the water.

In vain he kicked and struggled, clutching wildly at the thing that was strangling him. A purely instinctive cry of horror and alarm broke from his lips. It was answered by another, although he barely heard it; then, as suddenly as it had seized him, the grip relaxed, and in a half-drowning condition he became aware of a huge black bulk looming over him. Hands seized him by the collar and lifted him bodily out of the water; a moment later he was gasping like a stranded fish on a wooden deck.

In a flash he understood everything—the horse, the rope that had nearly throttled him, and the barge it was towing. He sat up hurriedly as the rays of a small oil lamp were turned on him. Behind it loomed vaguely the bulk of a human form.

'Thanks,' he said, with not a little confusion.

To his surprise, it was a female voice that answered him. 'We catch queer fish in the river these days,' it said.

'Queer fish?' At first Thirty did not understand. Then, looking down, he saw to his horror and dismay that the remains of his blouse had disappeared, leaving his uniform exposed. With a wild idea of jumping back into the river, he began scrambling to his feet, but a firm hand forced him back.

'*Ssh*,' hissed the woman. 'Lie still; we are nearly at the bridge.'

Thirty flopped back as a heavy piece of material smelling of tar was flung over him, thanking his lucky star that the woman was either French or, possibly, Belgian*.

He had little time for reflection, however. A few seconds later a curt challenge came out of the darkness. The barge drifted on sluggishly, while a conversation ensued with the sentry. Silence fell. The barge floated on. Thirty lay still.

Some minutes later his covering was removed.

The woman chuckled. 'I fooled those pig-dog Prussians,' she said vindictively. 'If you're the man they're looking for you're lucky I came along. Where are you going?'

'That doesn't matter, does it?' returned Thirty, evasively. 'Where are we now?'

'On the canal.'

That told Thirty nothing. He stood up. A quarter of a mile away a few scattered lights gave him the position of Belville. The aftermath of the storm had passed; the sky was clearing, and a swift examination of the stars that were visible told him that the barge was moving northward. 'I must get ashore,' he said. 'I'm going in the wrong direction.'

'Any direction will be the wrong one, I should think, if you walk about in those clothes,' observed the woman meaningly.

---

* He was, of course, in French territory occupied by the Germans.

'Are you here alone?' asked Thirty suddenly, wondering why the woman's husband had not appeared.

'My husband is at the war,' replied the woman, simply. 'Do you need clothes? If so, I have some.'

'A blouse, perhaps, or a big coat.'

'Wait.'

The woman was back in a few moments with an assortment of musty clothes.

Thirty selected an ancient oilskin coat, and put it on. 'Thank you, *Madame*,' he said quietly. 'You may have done more than you know for France.' He held out his hand. 'And now, if you will guide the barge a little nearer to the bank . . . ' Thirty indicated which one.

The woman put her weight against the rudder until the unwieldy vessel was within jumping distance of the bank. Thirty took a running jump and landed safely. '*Adieu, Madame*,' he called softly.

'*Bon voyage, M'sieur*\*,' came the reply, and the barge with its patriotic captain glided away into the darkness.

Thirty struck off across country in the direction of the road he knew, and after an unpleasant journey lasting more than half an hour, during which time he fell into more than one ditch, he reached it. To his relief it was deserted, and with the satisfaction in his heart of a job well done he set off at a trot for the landing-ground, anxious to reassure Rip, who he knew would be worried on his account.

He met two cars, but their headlights gave him ample warning of their approach, and he crouched in the hedge until they had passed.

\* French: Goodbye, Madame
   Have a good journey, Monsieur

He judged that it was not far short of daylight by the time he reached the rendezvous, but the old adage of the darkest hour coming before dawn appeared to be true in this case, and visibility was restricted to a few yards. He scrambled over the hedge of the actual landing-field, and then broke into a run alongside it, making for the place where he expected to find Rip, a relaxation of caution he was speedily to regret. Rounding a sharp corner, he came face to face with a man who was standing there. His height alone told him that it was not Rip. Before Thirty could collect his wits, the man had sprung upon him and hurled him to the ground.

Thirty fought like a wild cat. In the soaking turf and the darkness there was no question of technique. It was catch-as-catch-can, exercised to the limit. He fought only to escape, but his opponent seemed equally determined that he should not. Over and over they rolled, using hands, arms, legs, and teeth, sometimes crashing into the hedge, and at other times rolling over and over on the rain-sodden grass.

The end came with a curious suddenness. There was a swift beat of running footsteps.

'Is that you, Thirty?' came Rip's voice, crisp and hard.

Thirty managed to gasp a strangled 'Yes', for his adversary had an arm hooked round his throat. To his utter amazement the man answered, too.

'What's that?' he jerked out in a startled voice, in perfect English. He sprang to his feet.

'What the deuce . . . !' cried Thirty, jumping up.

'What's going on?' asked Rip, in such puzzled tones that Thirty almost smiled.

'Yes—what's going on?' cried the stranger, in a voice which showed that his amazement was as genuine as Rip's.

'What are you doing here?' demanded Thirty. 'Who are you?'

'Well, since we seem to be wearing the same uniform, I may as well tell you,' was the quiet answer. 'Captain Forsyth, Ninth Buffs. That's me. And I reckon we're here for the same reason.'

At last Thirty understood. He saw that in the struggle his oilskin had been nearly torn off his back, so that his tunic could be seen. 'You've come here hoping to be picked up?' he said.

'You bet I have. So have you, haven't you?'

'Of course.'

'Good! Now we all know where we are. Got a gasper?'

'No. I wouldn't permit smoking if I had.'

'What do you mean—you wouldn't permit?'

'I happen to be part of the organization that is running this rescue show,' retorted Thirty. 'How did you know about it?'

'Fellow named Smithson told me—stout fella, Smithson.'

'You've seen him—lately?' Thirty's voice was tense with excitement, for Smithson was the name Forty had adopted for his enterprise.

'Of course—else how could he tell me?'

'Where?'

'In the *Gefangenlager**.'

'Is he all right?'

---

* War prisoners' camp—usually referred to by prisoners by the German name.

'Right as rain.'

'Grand!'

The other hesitated a moment. 'Why are you so pleased about it?'

'Because he happens to be my brother.'

'Ah! I see. But the chief point is, how long do you reckon we shall have to wait here?'

'I don't know. Our plans have become slightly unstuck. I hope somebody will come over at dawn to pick us up, but whether or not there will be enough machines for all of us is more than I can say.'

'Well, if we can't all get in, you two had better go first, since you seem to have prior claims. I'll take my turn.'

'That's very decent of you,' declared Thirty. 'It is beginning to get light, I think, so we shall soon know.'

While they had been talking a rosy flush had been stealing upward from the eastern horizon. Thirty nodded towards it. 'Red morning, airman's warning,' he misquoted, little dreaming how apt his words were to prove.

# Chapter 16
# 'Captain Forsyth of the Buffs'

The minutes passed, the sky growing brighter, but still there came no comforting drone of aero-engines from the west. A lark appeared, trilling its way upward into the blue above the slight ground-mist that steamed from the wet earth.

Thirty got up from the bank on which they had, by common consent, decided to sit. 'I'm getting peckish,' he announced. 'I hid a bag of grub in this hedge a day or two ago, along there near the corner of the wood. I'll go and retrieve it. There is no need for us to starve. I'll come straight back if I hear a machine coming.'

With that he began to stroll quickly along the side of the hedge towards the wood, keeping a sharp look-out, although at such an early hour he did not expect to see any one. So quiet was everything, and so little need did there seem for vigilance, that his thoughts were miles away when, rounding a tall growth of bracken near the fringe of the wood, he came face to face with a German soldier.

The German had leaned his rifle against a stump, and was eating bread and sausage from a paper bag with the aid of a clasp-knife. He looked up as Thirty appeared. Over a distance of perhaps five or six yards their eyes met.

The effect on Thirty was of a violent electric shock. So utterly unprepared was he for anything of the sort that his brain was struck into a condition of paralysis. The muscles of his face froze into rigid lines as he stared.

The German, after a passing glance, went on casually eating his sausage.

'I'm mad,' was Thirty's first thought. 'I'm seeing things.'

The German looked up again, groped in his bag and produced another sausage. 'Have some?' he invited him.

Thirty found enough strength to shake his head. '*Danke\**,' he mumbled mechanically. His lips merely formed the word. Inwardly he was saying, 'No, he's mad, not me.' His eyes wandered on along the hedge. Twenty yards away another German began humming softly as he cleaned out his pipe with a stalk of grass. He nodded pleasantly when he saw Thirty looking at him.

'They cannot *both* be mad,' Thirty told himself desperately, swallowing something in his throat. 'What the . . . ?'

With his brain still reeling, he turned and began slowly to retrace his steps. In such a chaotic mental condition was he that he even looked down at the front of his uniform to see if in some miraculous way it had turned from khaki to grey. He saw that it was still khaki, and the discovery did nothing to elucidate the incredible incident. An uncomfortable sensation in the back made him look over his shoulder. Surely the Ger-

---

* Thank you

mans had realized their mistake by this time, and would be taking aim at him, he thought. But the bracken now hid them from view.

The sensation of unreality that he had experienced when he first found himself in France again swept over him, but he increased his pace and soon arrived back at the spot where he had left the others. They were still sitting on the bank, chatting.

Rip looked at Thirty's hands. 'Didn't you find the grub?' he questioned, in a disappointed voice.

'No,' answered Thirty, grimly, 'I didn't.'

'Why not?'

'Unless I'm crazy, there are Boche soldiers along there in that wood.'

Rip sprang to his feet. '*What!*'

Thirty shrugged his shoulders helplessly. 'There are soldiers along there.'

'But—did they see you?'

'Yes.'

Rip's face revealed his alarm.

'It's all right,' said Thirty in a peculiar voice, 'they are quite harmless.'

Rip stared at him. 'What are you talking about?' he muttered.

'He's pulling our legs,' smiled Forsyth.

'This is no time for fool tricks like that,' returned Thirty angrily. 'I tell you I saw two Huns along there— eating their breakfast.'

'Then it looks as if we're sunk,' declared Rip hopelessly. 'They'll get Biggles if he tries to land.'

'I shall light a fire and stop him; that was the arrangement,' retorted Thirty, bitterly.

Forsyth scrambled to his feet. '*Where* did you say these Germans were?'

'Along there by the wood. What are you going to do?'

'I'm going to have a look at them.'

'Don't be a fool.'

'I'll—'

'Hark!' broke in Thirty, tensely.

From far away, rising and falling on the now gently stirring air, came the low, vibrant hum of aero-engines. 'That's Biggles,' declared Thirty. 'That's a Beardmore engine, I'll swear. He must have got hold of a Fee. I'll light a fire.'

Forsyth ran a few paces along the hedge. 'What are you talking about?' he asked gruffly. 'There isn't a soul in sight.'

'Have you got a match?' asked Thirty, wildly.

'No.'

'Have you, Rip?'

'They're soaking wet.'

Thirty threw up his hands helplessly.

'Where are those Boches?' asked Forsyth. 'If there were any about we should see them moving now.'

Thirty ran to where he was standing and stared along the hedge and the edge of the wood. As Forsyth had said, there was nobody in sight.

'I give it up,' muttered Thirty. 'I could have sworn I saw Germans sitting—'

'Nerves,' broke in Forsyth. 'I've had that happen to me more than once. Fellows in the trenches are always shooting at Huns that don't exist.'

'You may be right,' returned Thirty, now seriously

164

beginning to wonder if he had been a victim of a hallucination.

There was no further time for conversation. From out of the western sky appeared four machines, two Camels and two dark-painted Fees. As they watched, Biggles's Camel, distinguishable by its wing-pennants, roared down low over the landing-ground, then zoomed up again.

Thirty ran into the open, waving furiously.

Instantly the propellers of the two Fees slowed down, and they began to glide in to land.

Thirty danced from one foot to the other in his excitement, glancing from time to time in the direction of the wood, for there was not the slightest doubt in his mind that if there *were* Germans there, their shots would reveal them. They could hardly remain passive while British aeroplanes landed within a hundred paces of them.

The first of the two Fees touched its wheels, bumped a little, and then ran to a standstill. The front cockpit was empty. Thirty dashed up to it. The pilot, his goggles pushed up, was grinning at him. He was a stranger to Thirty, but it was no time for introductions.

'There are three of us,' yelled Thirty. 'What shall we do?'

The pilot grimaced. 'I think I can manage two, but it will be a tight fit,' he replied. 'Grimsdon, my partner, will take the other. Hurry up.'

Thirty saw that Rip had run across to the other Fee, which had now landed. The two Camels were circling overhead.

'Get a move on,' shouted the pilot irritably.

'We'd better get in here,' Thirty told Forsyth, who

165

was standing beside him. Then he yelled to Rip to get into the other machine, with whose pilot he was now carrying on a conversation.

'Get in first, Forsyth. I'll sit on your lap,' muttered Thirty.

Forsyth swung himself up into the nacelle cockpit. Thirty followed, and squeezed himself on his lap. 'Off you go,' he shouted to the pilot, after satisfying himself that Rip had got into the other machine.

The take-off in the heavily loaded machine was a hair-raising affair. It was not so much the weight that mattered, because a machine that was designed to carry a 230-lb. bomb in addition to its observer, and other equipment, made light of Thirty's nine stone; but the weight was too far forward for the centre of gravity, with the result that the tail swung high and the nose nearly went into the ground, for which the pilot, unaccustomed to such unusual loading, could hardly be blamed. However, after an unpleasant swerve or two and an exceptionally long run, the machine staggered into the air, and after that there was no danger. A Camel soared up alongside, and Thirty found himself looking into Algy's smiling face.

They saw no enemy aircraft during the journey to the lines, in which they may have been fortunate, for, closely packed as Thirty was with Forsyth, it would have been impossible to manipulate the Lewis gun with which the cockpit was equipped. However, this may have been due as much to Biggles's foresight as to pure luck, for the presence of Mahoney, who met them with six Camels some distance over the lines, no doubt did much to keep the air clear.

Thirty had no recollection of the last part of the

trip. In spite of his efforts to prevent it, he dozed, the inevitable result of sheer weariness and nervous exhaustion after all he had been through during the night.

He came to with a start as the machine landed, and as soon as it came to a standstill he lost no time in vacating his cramped seat. The other Fee landed. Biggles and Algy walked over, and presently they all forgathered on the tarmac.

'I rather expected that Raymond would be here,' observed Biggles, looking round.

'Do you mind if we go down to the mess and have some breakfast?' asked one of the Fee pilots. 'If there's nothing else we can do—'

'By all means,' replied Biggles. 'Thanks, chaps, for your help. We shall be along ourselves presently.' He turned to Thirty as the two night-flying pilots strolled away in the direction of the officers' mess. 'How did you get on?' he asked eagerly.

'I delivered the goods,' Thirty told him, with a faint smile.

'Good show!'

'By the way, meet Forsyth,' continued Thirty. 'I found him waiting on the landing-ground for a lift home.'

Biggles shook hands with the infantry officer.

'I was mighty relieved to see you turn up,' Thirty told Biggles. 'You guessed we were in a mess, evidently.'

'I didn't exactly *guess*,' returned Biggles, lighting a cigarette and flicking the match away. 'When that frightful storm blew up as soon as you'd gone I reckoned you'd be lucky to weather it. Not only that,

I was pretty certain that if nothing went wrong you'd get off the ground before daylight. I waited here until it was daylight, and when there was no sign of you I thought we'd better come and have a look at things. We couldn't do any harm, anyway. The first thing I saw when we arrived was your burnt-out machine. That's all there was to it.'

'Where did the Fees come from?'

'From 100 Squadron. I tried to get a Bristol, but couldn't, so I rang up Shorty Grimsdon, of one hundred, and asked him to oblige, which, being a good scout, he did. But what are we standing here for? Let's go and sit down in the office. I'd say let's go down to the mess, but we'd better stick around for a minute or two in case Raymond turns up. I should have thought he would be here by now.'

'I'll go and ring him up, I think, and tell him every-thing is O.K.,' suggested Thirty, in a peculiar tone of voice.

'Yes, I should,' replied Biggles. 'By the way, are you all right?'

'Yes—why?'

'I thought you were looking a bit odd.'

'Tired, I expect.'

'I see. All right. You'll find us in the office.'

When Thirty rejoined the others a few minutes later they were sitting in the Flight Office, their flying-kit discarded. He flung his on its usual peg and pulled out a chair from under the small deal table on which lay their log-books.

'Well, I think I'll be getting along,' announced Forsyth.

'What's the hurry?' asked Thirty quietly.

'Oh, anxious to get back, you know. My C.O. will be pleased to see me.'

'I'd sit still if I were you,' went on Thirty evenly, his eyes on the other's face. There was such a curious inflexion in his voice that Biggles stared at him.

'No; if it's all the same to you, I'll push along,' mused Forsyth.

'It isn't all the same to me,' said Thirty in a voice that was as brittle as ice.

Forsyth turned sharply. 'What do you mean?'

'You'll sit where you are, that's what I mean,' grated Thirty.

There was dead silence. Every one in the room stiffened. In Thirty's hand was an automatic, its muzzle pointing unwaveringly at Forsyth's chest.

# Chapter 17
# A Life for a Life

The silence persisted for a full half-minute, during which time Thirty's eyes never left Forsyth's face. He saw the expression of cheerful carelessness fade, to be replaced by one of cold resignation.

'What the—?' Biggles's eyes went from the weapon in Thirty's hand to the mark at which it was levelled. He seemed to be at a loss for words.

'Biggles,' said Thirty, speaking very distinctly, 'a very curious thing happened at the landing-ground this morning. I did not understand it at the time, but I do now. But first let me direct your attention to the uniform the man who calls himself Forsyth is wearing. Coming home I sat very close to him, so close that I was able to perceive by the smell of his tunic that it has just been chemically cleaned. Since when have the Germans started cleaning their prisoners' uniforms for them, I should like to know? I know why *this* one was cleaned, though. If you will examine the front of that tunic very closely you will see that a small hole has been repaired. It isn't easy to see because it has been carefully done. It is just over the . . . heart. Just the sort of hole you might expect to be made by a . . . bullet. A bullet did go through that tunic—and it went through the heart of the man who was wearing it. I expect it was . . . Forsyth. Forsyth of the 9th Buffs. It made an ugly stain, that bullet . . . a stain that had to be rubbed hard with chemicals to remove it. But you can just see the edge of it.'

Thirty's voice went on inexorably. 'When I was waiting at the landing-ground I walked slap into a Boche. He gave me no more than a passing glance—a very different reception from what a British officer in enemy country might expect. Do you know why? I'll tell you. The Boche troops who were there *knew* that a . . . man . . . in a British officer's uniform, was waiting there, or due to arrive there, to be picked up.'

Thirty's eyes, cold and hard, stared into those of the man who called himself Forsyth. 'Am I right?' he asked.

The other did not answer.

'*Am I right?*' Thirty's eyes suddenly blazed, and the words left his lips with a vehemence that made the listeners jump.

The man he addressed drew a deep breath. He moistened his lips with his tongue. The muscles of his now ashen face twitched. 'Yes,' he said quietly. A ghost of a smile flitted over his face. 'Since we have passed the stage where denial might be of service, I might as well admit that—you are quite right.'

'You are a spy?'

The German moved his shoulders an inch. 'And what, sir, are you?' he asked softly.

Thirty caught his breath. 'That has nothing to do with it,' he answered icily.

Biggles broke in. 'Go and turn out the guard,' he ordered Rip, curtly.

'Wait!' cried Thirty.

Biggles raised his eyebrows. 'I am in command here,' he said, evenly.

'Yes . . . I'm sorry.'

Algy spoke for the first time. 'I think I know what Thirty means,' he said, quietly. 'The game is up. The Boche has tried to turn the tables on us. The landing-ground—for us—is now a trap.'

'I'm not thinking about the landing-ground,' cried Thirty, almost hysterically. 'Haven't you realized yet what this means? They've got Forty. They'll shoot him. They'll—'

'All right, pull yourself together,' broke in Biggles sharply. He turned to the prisoner. 'May I assume it is correct that your people have arrested Captain Smithson for espionage?'

'You may assume what you like,' was the calm reply.

Thirty handed his automatic to Biggles. 'Will you allow me to ask the prisoner—*my* prisoner—a few questions?' he demanded.

'Can it serve a useful purpose? This matter is now outside our hands.'

'It may,' returned Thirty. 'Nobody knows about this prisoner—yet.' He turned to the German, who was regarding him stolidly. 'You know that after you are handed over it will only be a matter of hours before you are shot?' he inquired, sharply.

'Of course. People who undertake *our* work must be prepared for that.'

Thirty ignored the oblique reference to his own activities. 'You would, I imagine, be interested in saving your life?'

'Naturally.'

'What are you getting at?' demanded Biggles.

'Please,' implored Thirty. He returned to the prisoner. 'I was thinking we might exchange a life for—a life,' he said in a low voice.

'You mean—exchange this fellow's life for Forty's?' asked Biggles.

'Yes.'

'But you can't do that sort of thing.'

'I'd do anything to save my brother—*anything*,' declared Thirty passionately.

The German started slightly at the words 'my brother'. 'Ah!' he exclaimed softly.

'You'll get yourself shot before you're through—in fact, all of us,' Biggles told Thirty grimly.

'Nothing of the sort. No one need know of this.' Thirty again addressed the prisoner. 'If we are going through with this we must understand each other,' he said. 'I am not asking you to betray your side. You need say no more than is necessary for me to save my brother's life. Neither side would gain anything if you both died; they would gain an advantage if you both lived. Is my brother a prisoner?'

'No.'

'Where is he?'

'No one knows. He escaped.'

'Did he know that his reason for being in your country was known to you?'

'Yes.'

'But you don't know where he is now?'

'We assume that he will make for the landing-ground where I was picked up.'

'And that is why the soldiers are there—to arrest him when he comes.'

'*So.*'

'And what part were you to play in this?'

'None. A means was provided for the department for which I work to place a man within your lines. I was chosen. The choice was not mine. I was a tutor of English at Heidelberg University. Also, I am able to fly.'

Thirty thought swiftly. It struck him that the man standing before him could not be known to the soldiers, or he, Thirty, would have been taken for an escaped prisoner when he came face to face with the German by the hedge. He realized now that the German soldier was prepared to see a British officer there, but could not recognize him personally. He proceeded to confirm it.

'The troops at the landing-ground do not know you by sight?'

'They have never seen me. I have never seen them.'

'They mistook me for you?'

'That is what occurred to me at once when you reported that you had seen a German soldier at close quarters, and he ignored you.'

'They were expecting you?'

'They had been warned, of course, that a man wearing a British uniform would be there, or would shortly arrive; otherwise my life would have been in danger.'

Thirty could now understand the whole situation. He went on swiftly.

'Were they told to expect one only, or how many?'

'I do not know that.'

Thirty felt that the man was speaking the truth.

'You say they are waiting for my brother. He will be in British uniform. How were they to know which was you, and which was him? Why did they not take me for him?'

'I can only suppose that when they saw a man strolling along the hedge in broad daylight they did not

174

imagine that it was an escaped prisoner. Therefore it must be me. They know now that I have gone. When another comes, perhaps creeping up the hedge, they will know it is the man they seek.'

'Ah! I understand. Do you know of the other landing-grounds?'

'We know everything. Your brother was suspected. A valuable British officer was placed in his cell with him—also a microphone was hidden in the wall.'

Thirty caught Biggles's eyes. 'We were afraid of that.'

Biggles shook his head. 'Really, Thirty, you can't go on with this,' he said. 'It's against all—'

'I don't care what it's against. Do *you* want to see Forty shot?'

'Of course not.'

'If no one ever knew about this, don't you think it would be a fair exchange?'

'Possibly.'

Thirty again turned to the German. 'It will save you the indignity of being searched if you will tell me truthfully whether you have any documents on you to prove your identity.'

The German smiled faintly. 'And me coming into the British lines? No.'

'A password, perhaps?'

The German hesitated.

'To withhold it will mean your death, and the death of another.'

'The password is—*Vorgehen*.'

'Advance?'

'*So*.'

Thirty turned to Biggles. 'That's all I want to know.'

'But what are you going to do, in heaven's name?'

'I'm going back to the landing-ground.'

'But it's trapped! It's stiff with soldiers.'

'I am quite aware of it. If I'm not back here in three hours you must take any steps you think proper. Look after the prisoner for me during that time. Maybe he will give you his parole.'

'And then?'

Thirty looked Biggles straight in the eyes. 'If I manage to get back here with Forty I shall allow *Captain Forsyth* to take a flight in the machine I come back in—which will be one of the F.E.'s.'

'You'll let him go?'

'What else?'

Biggles raised his hands, palms outward. 'I've nothing more to say,' he said in tones of resignation. 'I shall be the one who is shot before this affair is finished.'

Another thought came into Thirty's mind. 'How did you propose to get back to your side of the lines when you had done what you came to do?'

'I hoped to be able to borrow an aeroplane.'

'Didn't you fear that you would be shot down by your own machines?'

'My headquarters were not likely to overlook such an elementary point,' was the calm reply.

'What were you to do?'

The German took a large yellow silk handkerchief from his pocket. 'I should have tied that on the tail of the machine,' he explained.

'Your *Jagdstaffeln*\* know that mark?'

* German: squadron

176

'Yes.'

'By gosh! That's worth knowing,' put in Algy.

The German shook his head. 'The knowledge is of little service to you, otherwise I should not have told you. The colour and the position from which it is exposed are changed every week.'

Thirty took the handkerchief. 'I'm going now,' he said.

'Well, good luck,' replied Biggles.

'Aren't you going to take me?' cried Rip.

'No.' Thirty walked towards the door. As he did so it opened and Major Raymond came in.

'Ah! Here you all are,' he said cheerfully. His eyes swept the room and came to rest on the stranger.

Thirty felt that the room was spinning round him. He could think of nothing to say.

Biggles came to his rescue. 'Allow me to introduce a friend of mine,' he said, casually. 'Captain Forsyth of the Buffs.'

# Chapter 18
# Thirty Goes Back

To Thirty's unutterable relief the major merely nodded. "Morning, Forsyth,' he said. Then, to Thirty, 'Where are you off to?'

'I'm just going to see what I can do with a Fee, sir,' answered Thirty, truthfully.

'I see. Well, don't let me stop you. I was just passing, so I thought I'd look in. You've nothing to add to what you told me on the telephone this morning?'

'No, sir. Everything went off all right.'

'Well, from a conversation I have just had on the telephone' (the major's voice took on a meaning tone), 'I should hardly say that. But all's well that ends well, that's the chief thing.'

'You don't want me again for anything, sir?'

'No—not at present.'

'Then I'll be getting off in case the Fees are wanted.'

'Yes, I'll be getting along, too. Just one thing. Will you fellows dine with me at Wing Headquarters to-night?'

Biggles answered for all of them. 'Thanks very much, sir, we'd like to.'

'Fine; then that's settled. See you later.' The major hurried away.

Biggles wiped imaginary perspiration from his brow. 'These shocks will be the death of me,' he declared, sadly.

Thirty took a last look round the room. In his heart he did not expect to see any of the faces again. But he did not say so. With a brief 'Look after Forsyth' he turned on his heel and walked quickly to the nearest Fee, which the mechanics had just finished refuelling. He tied the handkerchief to the tail and then climbed into the cockpit.

His face was set in hard lines as he took off. He felt that he had reached the limit of something—he was not sure what. The crucial moment of his life was at hand. The next hour would decide his fate, and Forty's fate. That was all that concerned him. Hitherto he had regarded the war as something impersonal; something which was best regarded in the abstract. Now the war meant him and Forty. For the first time he began to perceive what war really meant; he felt the relentlessness of it—the ruthlessness, the waste, the cruelty, the incredible folly of it. It gave him a shock to realize that he did not really know what everybody was fighting for. Something about Belgium . . . Freedom. He pictured the face of the man who had called himself Forsyth; he was quite young, not much older than himself; he did not look as if he wanted to make a slave of anybody; a few months ago he was probably playing rugger; to-morrow he might be riddled with bullets. Yet only a short while before he, Thirty, had been impatient to get to the war. How silly it all was. A wave of despondency swept over him.

He was, of course, tired; more tired than he knew; yet, strangely enough, he was not conscious of it; on the contrary, he felt curiously alert. His brain thought clearly, intensely. It seemed to be racing inside his head. Every nerve in his body was keyed up, quivering like a taut wire in a gale. He could almost feel them vibrating. They made his hands tremble.

He found a piece of chewing-gum tucked into a slot in the instrument-board. He chewed it gratefully; there was something comforting about it, reminding him of school, and the things he knew and understood.

He started as a crimson Fokker triplane dropped out of the sky and whirled round him, banking steeply. The pilot raised his hand, and the machine swept away in a climbing turn, beautiful to watch as the sun flashed on its wings.

Thirty half smiled to himself. The yellow handkerchief was acting like a magic banner. He realized suddenly that he was not being archied, and again he knew the reason, finding time to admire the enemy's organization. A single order, a stroke of a pen, and an enemy machine was allowed to fly unmolested through skies that bristled with death. Amazing!

He flew on. One by one the landmarks that he had learnt to recognize slipped away behind him. A two-seater, camouflaged in a fantastic pattern of green and brown, which almost concealed the black Maltese cross on its side, passed him, going the other way; the leather-clad observer was leaning against his gun, his goggled eyes on the British machine. He did not move. The machine swept past and in a few moments was a speck in the distance.

Thirty leaned over the side of his cockpit and stared steadily ahead. He picked out Belville, a mere cluster of houses set in the green fields. He saw the church, and the silver ribbon that was the river on which, only a few hours before, he had floated on a barge with a woman whom he would never see again. What a strange thing war was, he reflected.

The wood which marked the position of the landing-field appeared out of the haze that shrouded the horizon. He regarded it calmly, although he knew that in a few minutes, when he landed beside it, his life would hang in the balance. He was mildly surprised to find that he felt no fear, although he had every reason for being afraid. For a moment he wondered why, but only vaguely; he was not really interested.

From a distance of not more than a quarter of a mile he subjected the field to an intense scrutiny. Not a soul was in sight. The wood, the fields around it, the hedges, revealed no sign of life. At some distance to the north a small herd of cattle was browsing in the shade of a spreading chestnut tree; otherwise the landscape was without movement as it basked in the summer sunshine. But Thirty was not deceived; he knew that within rifleshot many pairs of eyes were watching him. The watchers had not yet seen the yellow signal attached to his tail; nose on to the wood, it would be, of course, impossible, so he made an S turn with the deliberate intention of allowing them to see it. He also watched the hedges closely, thinking that he might see Forty, but no such figure could be seen, so, steeling himself to the perilous task ahead, he throttled back and glided in to a smooth landing.

Without waiting for the machine to run to a stop he opened the throttle again slightly and taxied towards the edge of the wood, swinging round so that the nose of the machine was pointing towards the open field.

He had given this matter of how to leave the machine considerable thought, for he wanted to be ready for a quick departure should it become necessary; but, on the other hand, he was most anxious not to do anything that might look suspicious. For the same reason he hesitated about switching off the engine, but in the end he did so, realizing that to leave it running would certainly invite comment. Then he jumped down and walked briskly towards the wood as if he knew quite well what it concealed. While he was still some yards away he hallooed loudly.

With an abruptness that startled him, a German officer, a *Leutnant*, stepped out of the bushes, followed by two or three soldiers, including the one whom he had seen eating his breakfast sausage earlier in the day. Inside the deep shade of the wood he could just make out the grey forms of more soldiers.

The presence of the man whom he had already seen gave him an unexpected opportunity of establishing his *bona fides**, which he was not slow in seizing. 'Finished your sausage?' he called, cheerfully.

The soldier grinned and nodded. '*Jawohl*****,' he said.

Thirty turned to the officer, but before he could speak the other addressed him. There was a look unpleasantly like suspicion in his eyes.

'Why are you here?' he asked, shortly.

'And why should I not be here?' demanded Thirty, coolly.

The German looked at the aeroplane, then back at Thirty. 'You are soon back.'

'I have to pick somebody up.'

'Pick somebody up?'

'Yes.'

* Credentials
** German: Yes

'I have received no such orders.'

'Well, I did, and that's all I'm concerned about.'

'May I remind you that you have not yet given the password?' returned the officer, stiffly.

Thirty gave it, and the other's manner relaxed.

'We have to be careful on this job, you know,' he explained.

'You'd be careful if you had *my* job, I can assure you,' returned Thirty, with a grin. 'Aren't you going to offer me some beer while I'm waiting for my man to arrive? You haven't seen him, by any chance?'

'What sort of man is he?'

'Something like me—a little older. But there, men in British uniforms can't be so common about these parts that there could be any mistake.'

The officer looked at Thirty with an odd expression on his face. 'What is his name?' he asked.

'I don't know his real name, and that's a fact,' admitted Thirty. 'We have no names, you know. The one I am to pick up will be called Captain Smithson where we are going.'

The German beckoned. Thirty followed, thinking that he was about to be offered some beer. He was quite unprepared for the shock awaiting him. Inside the wood, sitting on a fallen tree with his chin cupped in the palm of his hand, was Forty.

Thirty's brain reeled, yet he realized that everything now depended on Forty's behaviour. If he took his cue, all might yet be well, but if he failed . . .

Forty stared at his brother as though he had been confronted by a ghost. Still staring, he rose slowly to his feet.

Thirty greeted him easily, but with well-affected

puzzlement. 'My dear old boy, what on earth are you doing here like this?' he asked, speaking, of course, in German. Then, as if he suddenly understood the situation, he whirled round on the German officer and went on swiftly, without giving Forty a chance to speak. 'What is the meaning of this?' he demanded harshly. 'Am I to waste my time here through your blundering clumsiness? This matter is urgent. I am told to pick up a man here; I even ask you about him, yet you stand there like a fool, saying nothing. Well, if there is a row about the delay, you'll get the blame, not me.'

'But . . . he's under arrest.'

'Under *what*?' Thirty shouted the words.

'Arrest.'

'You're mad. This is the man I am to pick up.'

'Then why didn't he say so?'

'Do you suppose we go about shouting our plans to the world? He was quite right to say nothing, but if it had been me, I should. Why don't you read your orders?'

'I was told to look out for an escaped prisoner,' muttered the German, sullenly. 'I was told nothing about your coming back to pick up another man.'

Thirty snorted with disgust. 'No wonder things go wrong, when simple orders like these are bungled. All right. Say no more.' Thirty turned to his brother. 'Are you ready?' he asked.

'Yes, quite ready.'

Thirty's heart glowed with relief. Forty had taken the cue.

But the German had not finished. 'Why didn't you tell me you were expecting to be picked up?' he demanded of Forty.

184

'Because I wasn't anxious to be picked up, that's why,' growled Forty. 'I'm about sick of these jobs.'

Thirty regarded him coldly. 'If that's how you feel you'd better go and report to headquarters,' he snapped.

'You needn't trouble to do that,' put in the German. 'Here is Colonel Thonberg coming now.'

Thirty looked up. Coming down a path through the wood was a typical German of high rank, followed by his staff.

Forty sprang to the *Leutnant*. 'Don't tell him what I said,' he implored. 'If you do he'll have me shot.' Then, to Thirty, 'Come on, let's go before he can ask us why we are dallying here.' With a furtive glance in the direction of the staff officer he started off towards the machine.

Thirty threw a last word at the *Leutnant*, who seemed to be at a loss to know what to do. 'It would be better to say nothing at all,' he said, tersely; 'otherwise we may all get in a mess.'

The German nodded curtly.

Thirty waited for no more, but set off at a run towards the Fee, overtaking Forty just before he reached it. 'Swing the prop,' he hissed. 'Jump in when she starts. It's going to be touch and go.'

Forty did not answer. As Thirty scrambled swiftly into his seat he ran to the propeller, which, in the case of an F.E., is behind the engine. He dragged the big blade round and paused as it picked up the compression. 'Contact!' he yelled.

Thirty's hand was on the contact-switch but he seemed incapable of moving it. His eyes were fixed on

185

the far hedge over which a formation of Albatros Scouts was gliding.

A sudden outcry behind him brought him to his senses. Snatching a glance over his shoulder, he saw the German staff officer, followed by a crowd of soldiers, burst out of the wood.

'Contact!' he shouted hoarsely, knowing now that the lives of both of them depended on whether the engine started.

His relief when it did was such that for an instant his senses swam, and for one ghastly moment he thought his overwrought nerves had broken down and that he was going to faint. But the spectacle of Forty tumbling into the gunner's seat brought him round with a rush.

'Let her go!' yelled Forty frantically. 'What are you waiting for?'

Thirty bit his lip and shoved the throttle open. The engine roared, but the sharp crack of rifle shots could be heard above it. A shot tore through the fabric just above his head; another ripped a long splinter out of the interplane strut near his left arm; yet another smashed against the rudder-bar causing the now racing machine to swerve. Forty, who was standing up ramming a drum of ammunition on the gun, nearly went overboard; only by a desperate clutch at the side of the cockpit did he save himself.

To Thirty, as he pulled the joystick gently backward, the whole thing became a nightmare. His actions as he lifted the machine off the ground were made without thinking; they were purely mechanical. With dispassionate interest he saw the Albatroses fly past him. He became aware that Forty was aiming his gun, and struck him a violent blow to make him desist. He realized, of course, that Forty knew nothing about the yellow signal. To Forty's stare of anger and amazement he bellowed, 'Don't shoot,' knowing that if he did the German pilots would certainly return the fire.

Forty realized what was intended, even although the reason was something he could not be expected to understand. In any case, by this time the brightly painted machines had passed on.

Thirty, looking back, saw the leader glide in and land on the field he had just left. The others remained in the air, circling. He knew well enough what would happen, and he thought he had better acquaint Forty with the distasteful truth in case he had not realized it. Beckoning him to come nearer, he bellowed in his ear, 'They'll come after us.'

Answered Forty, 'And they'll catch us.'

Thirty nodded, and settled himself down for the race to the lines, making no attempt to climb, but keeping the joystick pressed forward so that the machine almost brushed the tops of the trees over which they passed.

# Chapter 19
# Through Thick and Thin

Thirty knew instinctively that the arrival of the staff officer in the wood had some direct bearing on himself, or Forty, or on both of them. That his mission was urgent was plain from the way he strode down the path. It was obvious, therefore, that half a dozen words with the *Leutnant* in charge of the vigilance party would be sufficient to reveal the true situation. It was equally obvious that the staff officer could order the Albatros *Staffel* to pursue them and spare no effort to destroy them. It was unfortunate that the Albatroses had arrived just at the critical moment, but it could not be helped. It was unreasonable, reflected Thirty, to expect the luck to be all on one side. On the whole things had gone as well as he could have hoped.

Forty was leaning out of his cockpit looking back under their tail. He drew himself in, caught Thirty's eyes, grimaced, and crossed his fingers—a common signal meaning 'Enemy aircraft'. Then he examined his gun.

Thirty did not trouble to look round. There was no need. Forty's signal had told him all there was to know. The Albatros *Staffel* was on their trail. He did not know the maximum speed of the Albatros, but he knew that it was a good deal higher than his own—which meant that the machines behind them would overhaul his own long before he reached the lines. 'Well, we can't do more than fight it out,' he thought, calmly.

It surprised him to discover how calmly he could regard the situation. His eyes were hot from strain, but his nerves were steady. He felt neither excitement nor fear; merely a smouldering hatred of his pursuers, of the enemy in general. They would kill him if they could. Very well, he would kill as many of them as possible before they succeeded in their design. That he and Forty would be killed he felt certain. It was too much to hope that one British machine, a rather slow, unwieldy two-seater at that, could fight a number of fast enemy fighters and survive. He was so sure of what the end would be that it did not worry him, so he was able to regard the immediate future quite dispassionately.

A line of enemy troops on the march on a main road below brought a faint smile to his lips. He was not more than fifty feet above them, so he could see their white faces clearly as they looked up. It was evident that at first they took it for granted that a machine so far over the lines must be one of their own, but when Forty's gun spat a hail of bullets into their close ranks their disillusionment was ludicrous to behold. A wild panic ensued, every man diving for such cover as offered. One or two, more courageous than the rest, flung up their rifles and fired at the intruder, but their aim was hurried, and if any of the bullets came near him Thirty was unaware of it. They tore on, leaving a scene of carnage and confusion on the white road to mark their passage.

Forty swivelled his gun round until it was pointing backwards and upwards over their top wing. He did not fire. Several times he took aim, swinging the muzzle from side to side as though trying to align it on a moving target. Thirty was only too well aware of the reason for this manoeuvre. The Albatroses were drawing in, creeping steadily into range; but they were old hands; they knew all about the deadly mobile gun in the front seat, and took care not to expose themselves. But this state of affairs did not last long.

Forty began firing short, sharp bursts, first on one side and then on the other. Something crashed into the engine with a violent *whang*.

Thirty touched his rudder-bar lightly, first with his left foot and then with the right. The movement caused the machine to swing slightly from side to side. He continued doing it, his intention being, of course, to spoil the enemy pilots' aim. It meant losing a little speed, but it was better than offering a 'sitting' target. He was still unable to see the enemy, but he knew perfectly well where they were. They were still behind him, and while they remained there both he and Forty were protected to a considerable extent by the engine. His greatest fear was that a bullet would hit the propeller, which would at once put the machine out of action. Thus crippled, they would have no option but to land and submit tamely to a fate he preferred not to contemplate.

A hail of bullets striking the machine somewhere in the rear made him kick the rudder-bar violently. He shoved the joystick forward viciously until his wheels were almost on the ground, a position of advantage of which he had heard other pilots speak. A machine diving on him from behind would have to be pulled out much sooner than if he was at a greater altitude, the reason being the risk of diving into the ground.

A belt of fir-trees forced him to zoom up again. He knew the trees. They formed one of his landmarks, and his heart sank a little as he realized that they were only half-way home. Another burst of bullets struck the machine like a gigantic cat-o'-nine-tails. He flinched instinctively, and then bit his lip as Forty went down in a heap. But he was up again in an instant, shaking his head to Thirty to show him that he was unhurt. He flung an empty ammunition-drum overboard. There was a jagged hole through the middle of it, and Thirty realized that a bullet had hit it as Forty was taking it off the gun; hence the fall.

A movement on the right caught Thirty's eyes, and he turned sharply in time to see the shark-like body of an Albatros zoom high in front of him. It roared up in a steep stalling turn, hung for a moment on top of the turn, and then came down like a meteor, orange flame spurting from the twin guns on the engine-cowling.

Forty's gun swung up to meet it, a new drum in place. The drum starting jerking round as the bullets left the muzzle.

Thirty watched the Albatros. He could see the tracer bullets from Forty's gun hitting it: they seemed to be going right through the fuselage: but still it came on, guns chattering like castanets. He clenched his teeth. One or the other could not fail to be hit if the enemy pilot did not soon pull out. A dreadful horror swept through him that the German intended ramming him, and he almost flung himself forward on the joystick.

The Albatros did not pull out. Thirty ducked and flung up his left arm to protect his face as the wheels skimmed over his head. It never did pull out. Thirty heard the crash above the roar of his engine as it sped, nose first, into the ground. He saw the flash of light, almost like lightning, as the petrol tank exploded. In a few seconds it was far behind.

Thirty's eyes came to rest on Forty's face. It fascinated him. It was white. His eyes blazed. His lips could hardly be seen, so close were they pressed together. They were just a straight line. 'So this is war,' he thought. Could it be possible that the man in front of him was the careless laughing boy he knew at school?

But more bullets were hitting the machine. They were coming from both sides now, as well as from above, in spite of his manoeuvring to prevent it. He realized that the machine was being shot to pieces about him; that the end *must* come at any moment. It was amazing that the machine had hung together as long as it had. For the first time he looked back. The air was full of machines. It seemed that several more had joined his original pursuers. And as he looked at them an emotion he had never before experienced surged through him. He did not stop to wonder what it was. He was conscious only of a sudden overwhelming fury, a blind hatred of the crowd of painted devils who were making a target of him. Well, he would show them.

A wild yell left his lips as he dragged the joystick back into his right thigh, at the same time kicking on full rudder. The machine soared up and round like a rocket, straight into the thickest of his enemies. What cared he if he collided with them? And collide with them he nearly did. Wings and wheels flashed past his face as, in a vertical bank, he plunged through startled

German machines. That there was no collision was due to them, not to Thirty. He let out another yell as Forty tore an empty drum from the gun and hurled it at a machine as it roared past him not more than twenty feet away. Madness seemed to have come upon him. Again he swung the Fee round, and deliberately chased the now turning Albatroses.

What he would have done next had he been alone, or had he been flying with a partner as hot-headed as himself, would be pure conjecture. Probably he would have completely lost his head, and in a berserk rage succeeded in ramming one of the enemy machines— which would have been the end of the affair. As it was, Forty had something to say about this crazy behaviour.

He climbed up on to his seat, not without some risk of falling out of the machine altogether, and struck Thirty a blow on the chest. 'What do you think you are doing, you lunatic? Get home—home—HOME.'

As he was in front of Thirty the slipstream carried the words back to him. In any case, the expression on Forty's face brought him to his senses. 'I'm mad,' he thought. 'I must try to get home.'

But it was easier said than done. Again came the nerve-shattering *flack-flack-flack* of bullets hitting his machine, so in desperation he took the only possible course if they were to escape annihilation: he threw the Fee into a steep bank.

An Albatros swept across his nose, black smoke pouring back from its engine, and the pilot, left arm over his face, raised himself high to escape the fumes. 'That's queer,' mused Thirty in a detached sort of way, for he had no recollection of Forty shooting at it. He saw two other black-crossed machines turning away. The

193

bullets had stopped. He sensed a change. Something was happening, but what was it? He craned his neck this way and that in his anxiety, surveying the atmosphere in all directions to try to find out what it was. Then a Camel flashed across his field of vision and he understood. His heart leapt, and he let out a yell of exultation. Camels! He and Forty were no longer alone. He started to turn to see more of the new-comers, but once more Forty's furious hammering restored his common sense.

'Get home, you fool,' shouted Forty.

Realizing the wisdom of his brother's advice, Thirty turned towards the lines, and putting his nose down raced for safety. He saw nothing of the dog-fight that raged at the spot where the Camels had joined issue, but he could well imagine what was going on. Several times he saw an odd Camel near him, and presently recognized it as Rip's machine. He also saw an Albatros some distance away; it paid not the slightest attention to him, having more pressing matters to engage its attention.

Not until they were nearly to the lines did he become aware of Biggles's Camel, recognizable by its pennants, flying just above him. Another joined it; several more were in the near distance, all heading for the lines. Long, winding communication trenches appeared below, then shell-holes in ever increasing numbers, and he knew that a few more minutes would see them safely home. Nevertheless, a burst of archie just in front of him warned him that he was not yet out of danger, for he was flying very low. Still, he knew that it would be even more risky to lose speed by climbing for height, so in order to spoil the gunners' aim he started zigzagging, a manoeuvre he kept up until the tangle of barbed wire and debris underneath told him that he was crossing the ghastly area of no-man's-land. Forty emptied what ammunition he had left into the enemy trenches as they raced across the lines to safety.

They were across. Thirty could hardly believe it. It did not seem possible. And then, with the relaxation of nerves that followed the knowledge that they were safe, came the inevitable reaction— a feeling of intense depression and utter weariness. All the strength in his body seemed to run down his legs and then disappear, leaving them weak and trembling. He could have cried—easily. He wanted to go to sleep at once. If only he could sleep! Never before had he wanted to go to sleep as he did now. It seemed the most desirable thing on earth, and only by a great effort of will did he keep himself awake.

He saw the aerodrome just in front of him. It appeared to float towards him, mistily. It did not look real. Nothing seemed real. The whole thing was a dream. Of course it was, he thought drowsily. He was dreaming. Presently he would awake and find himself back at school . . . how very pleasant that would be . . .

'Steady—what are you doing?' yelled Forty.

Thirty started convulsively, realizing with a shock that he had nearly fallen asleep at the joystick. He struck his knees violently with his clenched fists to wake himself up; then, bracing his sagging muscles, he throttled back and started to glide in. The aerodrome seemed to rush up towards him, and he drew the stick back, only to push it forward again as the machine staggered drunkenly on the brink of a stall. A horrible feeling came over him that he was going to crash. The earth was sinking away under him now, and automatically he eased the stick forward to overtake it. Instantly his wheels struck it with a crash; the machine bounced high, came down with another violent bump, and finally settled down in the worst landing he had ever made in his life. He didn't care. He didn't care about anything. Still, he taxied up to the sheds before he switched off. Not until then did he sink back with a deep sigh that was something more than mere relief. He sat quite still. He did not want to get out. He only wanted to sit where he was and enjoy the silence . . . the peace . . .

Forty struck him a friendly blow on the arm. 'Come on, old boy,' he said, breezily. Then, with anxiety rising in his voice, 'You're not hit, are you?'

'No,' murmured Thirty, with a foolish smile. 'Just tired. I was just . . . sort of . . . getting my breath.' Nevertheless, he allowed Forty to help him down to the ground. He shook himself and made an effort to pull himself together when he saw Biggles hurrying towards them.

'Good show, kid,' he said, cheerfully, slapping Thirty on the back. 'I should say that is the best bit of individual work that has been done since this perishing war started, and I've seen some pretty stout efforts, too.' Then, with a change of voice, he asked, 'What are you going to do about Forsyth?'

Thirty blinked. The words seemed to act on him like an electric shock. 'Forsyth! My gosh! Yes . . . I'd forgotten all about him,' he gasped. 'Where is he?'

'In the Flight Office, I expect. At least, I hope so. I left him there with Flight-Sergeant Smyth.'

'But why did you leave him? You said . . . '

196

'I know,' muttered Biggles. 'But to tell you the truth, I got jolly worried after you had gone. It seemed to me that you were bound to run into trouble. I couldn't just sit still and do nothing, so I collected everybody I could find and came across to see what was going on.'

'Good thing you did,' declared Forty. 'We should never have got home otherwise, that's certain. We were properly up against it. Thirty went completely off his head when the Huns caught us—barging about the sky as if he was flying a tank instead of an aeroplane. Who's this fellow Forsyth you're talking about? What's he done?'

'You ought to know,' answered Biggles quietly. 'I'll tell you all about it presently—it's a long story. Come and meet him. I expect he'll still be in the office with Smyth.'

They all made their way slowly towards the building. Just outside the hangar they waited for Algy to join them, after which they all went on again.

As they approached the Flight Office Biggles went on in front. With his hand on the door-knob he turned to Thirty. 'What are you going to do about him?' he asked.

'You know what I promised,' replied Thirty in a low voice.

'But you can't do that now.'

'Why not?'

'Think.'

Thirty struggled to understand what Biggles meant. Then the truth burst upon him.

'Of course!' he cried. 'The signal is no more use.'

'Exactly. Any one flying that machine of yours over

the lines now would have a pretty thin time. I'll warrant every machine within fifty miles is looking for it.'

Thirty's face fell. 'What on earth are we going to do about it? I must live up to my promise.'

'We shall have to tell Forsyth what has happened, that's all,' declared Biggles. With that he opened the door.

For what might have been a matter of three seconds he stood still, staring into the room. The others, realizing that something was wrong, crowded behind him and pushed him into the room. 'What do you think about that?' he said in a hard voice.

There was no need for him to add an explanation to his question. On the floor, just raising himself on his elbow and looking dazed, was Flight-Sergeant Smyth. There was an ugly swelling between his eyes. The window, which opened on to the side of the hangar, was pushed right back. Of the German there was no sign.

'He's gone,' snapped Biggles. 'The skunk has broken his parole.'

'No!' cried Algy. 'Technically he was within his rights. He gave *you* his parole—you personally—not Smyth.'

'Technicalities my foot!' snarled Biggles. 'Morally he should have waited. Let's see if we can—' He broke off as the deep-throated roar of a Beardmore engine suddenly shattered the quiet of the aerodrome.

Biggles said nothing. With a sweep of his arm he thrust Algy aside and dashed through the hangar to the aerodrome. Reaching it, he pulled up dead and threw up his hands helplessly. 'There he goes,' he said.

'Hi! What do you think you are going to do?' he went on quickly, as Thirty started running forward.

'I thought perhaps in a Camel I could—'

'Could what? The only way you could stop him would be to shoot him down, and you can't very well do that. You said you would let him go. Well, he's gone. Let him go. His blood is on his own head—not ours.'

*Bang! Bang! Bang!* The anti-aircraft gun on the far side of the aerodrome suddenly opened up.

*Whoof! Whoof! Whoof!* Like a distant echo came the explosion of the bursting shells. Three puffs of white smoke appeared in the sky.

'What are they shooting at?' cried Biggles in a bewildered voice. Not unnaturally, he was still watching the Fee in which the German had escaped. Already it was half a mile away, making for the lines, but there was no archie smoke near it.

'Look!' ejaculated Algy sharply, and pointed.

Simultaneously the air was filled with noise as three Albatroses, which must have been gliding at a great height overhead with their engines throttled back, plunged down in a steep power dive in the wake of the F.E.

A cry of horror broke from Thirty's lips, but nothing was said.

Breathlessly, the watchers on the tarmac waited for the end. But it was decreed that they should not see it. The F.E. grew dim, and then disappeared from sight in the summer haze that hung over the distant landscape. The three German machines plunged into it too, and a moment later were swallowed up. From far away, so far that they could only just hear it, came the mutter of a machine-gun. The drone of the engine died away. Silence fell. High up in the blue a lark began to warble.

'They've got him,' muttered Thirty in a dull voice.

'Not necessarily,' returned Biggles, quietly. 'If he was quick he might have got down.'

'If I thought he was killed—'

'Why worry? What he did he did himself. You've nothing to blame yourself for.'

'I can't help feeling—'

Biggles put his hand on Thirty's shoulder. 'I think you've forgotten something,' he said quietly.

'What?'

'This is war. We are all in it. His turn to-day; ours, maybe, to-morrow. In war there is neither forgiveness nor compassion. We're—'

'What's going on?' interrupted a well-known voice.

As one, the watchers swung round. Major Raymond was standing behind them.

'What are you all staring at?' he inquired curiously. 'I can't see anything.'

'There is nothing to see, sir,' answered Biggles, casually. 'We were just watching a machine take off, that's all.'

The major nodded. 'Come over to the Squadron Office, you fellows, will you? I want a word with you,' he said in an official tone of voice.

Obediently they all followed him as he led the way.

# Chapter 20
# Accused

Major Mullen, the C.O., was sitting alone at his desk when they trooped into the Squadron Office, Major Raymond first, conspicuous by the scarlet tabs on the lapels of his tunic, followed by Biggles, Algy, Forty, Rip, and Thirty.

Major Raymond looked at the C.O. 'Shall I say it or will you?' he asked quietly.

'It's more a matter for Wing than for me, so I'd rather you did,' returned Major Mullen.

Major Raymond turned to Thirty. 'A rather curious thing has happened,' he began, in that suave tone of voice that senior officers know so well how to adopt when it suits their purpose. 'In view of the excellent work you have done since you joined this squadron, and more particularly for the special mission which you carried out successfully for me, I submitted your name to General Headquarters for a decoration—the Military Cross, to be precise.'

Thirty guessed what was coming. He felt the muscles of his face stiffen, and something seemed to sink inside his stomach. He did not know how he knew, but he *knew*. He did not speak.

'You can imagine my surprise,' continued the major, 'when Wing Headquarters were informed by General Headquarters, who had been in touch with the Air Board, that there was no officer of your name on the list of the Royal Flying Corps. Not unnaturally we assumed that you had been seconded from another regiment, but there was no record of that either. When we discovered that there were *two* officers at this unit not appearing on the official list, we felt that it was time we made inquiries. Naturally, we asked your C.O. for the movement orders you would normally present on arrival; he thereupon told us that you had arrived without any. Can you offer any explanation of the strange state of affairs?'

Thirty swallowed something in his throat. 'I can, sir,' he said in a low voice.

'Well?'

'The fact of the matter is, sir, we . . . er . . . that is—'

'I'm waiting.'

'Well, we're not officers at all; that is, we've never been gazetted,' burst out Thirty, desperately.

'*What?*' The word came from Forty. His lips continued to move, but no words came. He appeared to have difficulty in speaking.

'It's true,' said Thirty, miserably.

'Where did you get those uniforms?' asked the major sternly.

'From my brother's wardrobe, sir.'

Forty's eyes grew round. 'What the—?'

The major interrupted. 'Just leave this to me, Captain Fortymore, will you?' He turned again to Thirty. 'Kindly continue,' he said, smoothly.

'I've nothing more to say, sir.'

'Why did you do this?'

'Because I wanted—we both wanted, but I was the ringleader—to get to the war.'

'But there are regular channels for that. I understand you both arrived here in service aeroplanes? Where did you get them?'

'We borrowed them, sir.'

'Stole them, you mean.'

'No, sir,' denied Thirty. 'We only moved them from one place to another. They've been in service all the time. We could think of no other way of getting here.'

'What was the hurry?'

'Well, Forty—that is, Captain Fortymore, my brother—was missing, and I hoped to be able to rescue him. And I did, too,' concluded Thirty, firmly.

The major stroked his chin. His face was still stern, but there was a twinkle in his eyes. 'You ran away from school?' The question was really a statement.

Thirty realized then that the major knew more than he pretended. 'Yes, sir,' he admitted.

'What do you suppose Germany would say if she knew?'

'I don't know, sir, and I don't particularly care,' declared Thirty. 'I got Forty—I mean, Captain Fortymore—back, and that's all I care about.'

'You've been a civilian under arms, liable to be shot if you were caught.'

'I should have been shot anyway if they had caught me,' Thirty pointed out, with truth.

The major coughed and caught the C.O.'s eyes. 'Yes, I suppose you would,' he conceded. 'But that does not alter the case. It was a most dangerous thing to do.'

'So was my trip to Belville the other night, sir, but you didn't stop me going on that account,' murmured Thirty.

'That was an entirely different matter.'

'Yes, sir—so I believe.'

'At your age you should have known better.'

'I did know, sir, but it made no difference. I succeeded in what I set out to do, so to apologize and say
I am sorry would be sheer hypocrisy. All the same, sir,
I apologize to you personally for the trouble I have
caused you. Also to the C.O. for deceiving him.'

'That sounds a ham-fisted sort of apology to me,'
observed the major. 'Still, I'll accept it. And what do
you think you are going to do now?'

'That is for you to decide, sir.'

'I suppose we ought to send you back to school.'

'Without wishing to appear boastful, I think I should
be of more use out here, sir.'

The major smiled. 'Algebra would seem a bit dull
after what you have been doing, no doubt,' he
remarked. Then his manner became serious again.
'Now look here, young man; this escapade of yours has
given General Headquarters—and the squadron for
that matter—a lot of trouble. In the circumstances
there is only one thing we can do. We cannot have
civilians walking about in uniform, so you have both
been given commissions in the field. Your names will
both appear in to-morrow's *Gazette*, and to save your
skins, in case either of you is ever caught by the enemy,
your commissions have been antedated from the day
you joined the squadron. Which means that you have
both been officers since that day. That being so, the
recommendation for the Military Cross has been
allowed to stand.'

Thirty could hardly believe his ears. 'Well, that's
frightfully good of you, sir,' he stammered. 'You may

be sure I shall—both of us will, in fact—try to live up to it.'

'If you go on as you have started we shall be satisfied.' The major smiled and held out his hand. He turned to Forty. 'You'd better keep an eye on this young brother of yours,' he said. 'I've spoken to Major Mullen about it; he says you can stay here in 266 if you like. Either that or you can take him with you to your old squadron.'

'I'm not going to leave Biggles,' announced Thirty, firmly.

'Well, talk it over,' smiled the major, making for the door. 'Oh, by the way, that dinner to-night is still on. Half-past seven, sharp.'

The C.O. accompanied the major to the door. For a moment or two they stood outside, conversing in low tones, before Major Raymond broke off and turned back to the office. 'Oh, there is one more thing I must tell that young rascal—' He stopped abruptly. 'Well,' he exclaimed, 'what do you think about that?' He raised his finger and pointed.

Thirty was slumped down in the C.O.'s chair. His eyes were closed. From his lips and nose issued a sound of deep, regular breathing. He was, in fact, fast asleep.

Major Raymond regarded him for a moment in silence. Then, 'In your chair, too, Mullen,' he said in a low voice. 'It looks to me as if it might be a case of coming events casting their shadows before.'

'There are more unlikely things than that,' said Biggles softly. 'Fetch a stretcher, Algy; let's put him to bed. In fact, I think it's about time we all had a spot of sleep.'

With which suggestion the others agreed.